SWEET NIG.

In the year 1594, B ⎯ ⎯ttering, a Member of Parliament and a Justice of the Peace, was growing tired of the capricious ways of his ward, John Harcourt. At the age of six, John had become the fifteenth Baron Harcourt de Laleham, under the joint guardianship of his mother and Bernard, his second cousin. John grew up spoilt and indulged by his mother, and after her death Bernard decided to bring his nineteen-year-old ward into line. When John falls in love with Tamsin, an illegitimate girl from a notorious family, Bernard is livid — and the affair is doomed . . .

SHEILA BISHOP

SWEET NIGHTINGALE

Complete and Unabridged

ULVERSCROFT
Leicester

First published in Great Britain

First Large Print Edition
published 1996

British Library CIP Data

Bishop, Sheila
    Sweet nightingale.—Large print ed.—
Ulverscroft large print series: romance
1. English fiction—20th century
2. Large type books
I. Title
823.9'14 [F]

ISBN 0–7089–3642–3

Published by
F. A. Thorpe (Publishing) Ltd.
Anstey, Leicestershire
Set by Words & Graphics Ltd.
Anstey, Leicestershire
Printed and bound in Great Britain by
T. J. Press (Padstow) Ltd., Padstow, Cornwall

This book is printed on acid-free paper

FOR
JANE

April

THE man at the table sat with his back to the window; if he had turned his chair, he would have been tempted to look out. The window ran up the whole height of the wall; between the panes the slender parallels of stone divided the view into segments, like the holy pictures on a Florentine chest. In the rapt solitude of early morning and early spring, Minton Gabriel looked like Eden before the fall.

Beyond the evergreen hedges of the formal garden, the grass was swept with gold where the lent lilies, their small trumpets double-frilled, crowded towards the stream. On the opposite bank there were ewes nibbling the new, sweet grass in the water-meadows, with their lambs tumbling around them. The ground drove steeply upwards to the ridge that divided the neighbouring combes of Minton and Sutleigh. It was densely covered with trees that were still bare, but the sap had risen in their veins, and branches that had been like wrought iron a month ago now seemed as delicate as lace.

Bernard Kettering knew this scene by heart, every acre of it was his own property, and he loved it with a single-minded passion, but nine o'clock in the morning was no time for indulging in Arcadian fantasies. He was checking through his household accounts, while his steward and his secretary stood waiting in a respectful silence.

Kettering flipped over a page of foolscap and encountered another list of figures. He was thirty-seven years old, a lean, powerful man with strong features and a faintly sardonic expression. He had been born in this house while his father was still building it, and had progressed through the usual stages of a gentleman's education: Oxford, the Middle Temple, and a spell in the Army. He had been knighted on the field of Zutphen eight years ago. Now, in 1594, he was dividing his time between the Court in London and his West Country estates, serving as a Member of Parliament and a Justice of the Peace.

Having finished his steward's neat audit, he put it down, and began to study a summary of day-to-day expenditure drawn up by his secretary.

"What's this item here at the end of the month?"

Edmund Royden jumped slightly and brought his attention back into focus.

Looking over his master's shoulder, he remarked helpfully, "It says twenty-one crowns."

"Yes, I can see it says twenty-one crowns. It doesn't explain what you did with them."

Royden shot an appealing glance at the steward, Mr. Creed, who took no notice.

Kettering made a sharp movement of exasperation. "I suppose they were for my cousin?"

"Well, sir — I didn't care to refuse — "

"Go and find his lordship, will you, Edmund? And ask him to do me the honour of waiting on me. Immediately."

"Yes, sir."

As Edmund left the room, the steward said in a deprecating way, "It's not easy for any of us to refuse Lord Harcourt."

"I know. That's what makes me so angry."

Kettering tapped a tune with his finger-nails on the edge of the table, staring at the door.

The young man who came in a few minutes later had a kind of physical poise and splendour that was almost aggressive. He was over six foot tall and very slim, but so well-proportioned that already, at nineteen, he had long out-grown any coltish awkwardness. He carried his head well, the dark brown hair was as smooth as polished wood, and his eyes were dark too: a very deep smoky blue.

He walked straight up to the table, and said: "I'm sorry if I've set the counting-house by the ears. I asked Royden to advance me some money last week, and then forgot to tell you."

"Forgot, John?"

"Certainly," said the boy glibly. "You know how it is — "

"Only too well." Kettering leant back in his chair, one hand on each of the carved arms. "You never had the smallest intention of telling me. You traded on your position to give orders to a member of my household, and hoped that it would be a long time before I found out."

"That's not true, sir — "

Kettering quelled him with a cold eye. "In case you should 'forget' again, I am going to acquaint these two gentlemen with the facts." He glanced from Creed to Edmund Royden. "While Lord Harcourt was in London, he managed to get through a whole quarter's allowance in a fortnight, since when he has been living on his credit. I have settled his debts, and for the present he will have to come to me for every penny he needs. There's to be no more borrowing. So if he applies to either of you again, you will know what to say."

There was a murmur of assent. Both men looked thoroughly uncomfortable, and Kettering, taking pity on them, let them go; he had finished all the business he meant to do that morning.

John Harcourt waited impatiently while they withdrew. He was trembling with mortification.

"Did you have to do that?" he burst out. "In front of your servants? Did you

5

have to haul me up like a schoolboy in disgrace, and let them know what I'd done and how I was being punished for it? You promised me that no one should know."

"No one need have known, if I hadn't caught you wheedling money out of my secretary behind my back. I don't think you deserve any particular leniency after that."

John tugged at his starched ruff as though it was too tight for him. "Is it a crime to ask for money that I can well afford to pay back? Even you will admit that I'm hardly a pauper, sir."

"In other words," paraphrased Kettering softly, "You could buy me up three times over, so you fancy that gives you a right to help yourself to whatever you please."

"I never suggested anything of the kind — "

"I'm glad to hear it. Now listen to me, Harcourt. You and I know certain circumstances that I didn't repeat to Creed and Royden. When I fetched you down from London last week, you had not merely wasted your money, you'd

6

misbehaved yourself at Court, got into a scandal with a married woman and into a brawl with her husband, and you have to be thankful to Sir Robert Cecil that the whole story didn't reach the Queen. Sir Robert has more important things to do than keeping sprigs of the nobility out of prison. He advised me to take you away until you knew how to conduct yourself properly."

The prodigal stood scowling at the floor. "Sir Robert didn't say I had to be mewed up here all the summer. If I'm to be exiled from London, couldn't I go to my own house at Crossingbourne? Or to Laleham?"

"Is it likely that I should allow you to set up on your own at your age? Especially after what happened in London."

"For heaven's sake, sir! There won't be any repetition. I don't make the same mistakes twice."

"Neither do I," said Sir Bernard. "From now on I'm not letting you out of my sight. I gather you find this house a poor substitute for Crossingbourne or Laleham. Nevertheless, it's the best we can offer, so I hope you don't mean to make it intolerable for the rest of us."

Somehow he always found himself taking this tone with John — using sarcasm like a whip.

He might not always get the result he wanted, but this time it was swift and total. The boy looked up, his sulking egotism pierced by a sudden contrition.

"I spoke without thinking — what an ungrateful churl I must have sounded, and on top of all the trouble I've caused you. Forgive me, sir." There was a whole-hearted simplicity about this apology that was hard to resist. "You and my cousin Ann are so good to me, and it's much more than I deserve."

"My dear John, there's no need to talk of deserving," retorted Sir Bernard, who was really very fond of him. "We are always glad to welcome you, and you'll find plenty to do here at Minton. Well, I've done preaching at you for one morning; high time I was out and about."

He got up briskly, still talking as he crossed to the door. Having opened it, he waited automatically for the younger man to pass through ahead of him. It was such an instinctive gesture that neither of them noticed it; as a guardian, he exercised a pretty stern authority over his ward, while still observing the ceremonial marks of respect due from a commoner to a peer of the realm. Thus adding one more ingredient to an already difficult situation.

Bernard Kettering and John Harcourt were second cousins. John's mother, Mary Kettering, had made an extremely good marriage. Her husband, the sole descendent of two ancient families, had died of fever at thirty-one, leaving his little son of six to succeed him as the fifteenth Baron Harcourt de Laleham, heir to vast wealth and lands which had been accumulating for nearly four centuries. Since the other male Harcourts were a raffish and unsatisfactory crew, the child had been left to the joint guardianship of his mother and his cousin Bernard. This meant that for twelve years Bernard had faithfully nursed the family fortunes, while he and Lady Harcourt had bickered continually about the heir. Bernard had sensible ideas about bringing up the boy who was going to inherit such immense responsibilities and temptations. Young John greatly admired his dashing soldier cousin, and would have been perfectly amenable — if he hadn't been so spoilt and indulged by his mother and her rather foolish second husband. She had died a year ago, so that Bernard now had complete control of his ward; he sometimes wondered if it had come too late.

"I can keep John in order when I've got him under my thumb," he remarked to his wife later that morning. "But let him get away for a few weeks, and it's all too easy for him to slip back into the habits he grew up with. Oh, I'm not saying his mother had any real vice in her, but she was self-seeking and careless and vain, faults which are so peculiarly dangerous to a young man placed as he is. He will find far too many people willing to gratify them."

"Poor John," said Ann Kettering. "Pursued by those impudent harpies at the Court, who give him no peace; small wonder he hasn't always been a perfect Galahad."

She was a pretty young woman of

twenty-six with the fair hair and blue eyes that were so much in fashion. Her formidable husband had married her for love when she was fifteen, and she had spent most of her time since then bearing his seven children. She was entirely singleminded and good — and yet, in her own particular way, just as susceptible to John Harcourt's charm as the ladies she despised so thoroughly. Kettering glanced down at her with a touch of amusement.

They were strolling along one of the gravel paths that ran at right angles through the chessboard regularity of the garden. On their left the great house of Minton Gabriel stood pale and magnificent against the rising slope of the combe. The front was broken by a series of projecting oriels that rose the full three storeys to the roof with its little forest of cupolas. There were sixty-five windows on the south front, mirrors of the clear sunlight, and the walls themselves had that faint, warm flush of apricot belonging to the stone which was dug three miles away in Minton Quarry, and nowhere else in England.

At the boundary of the ornamental garden Bernard and Ann leant on the low wall and looked over. There was a patch of rough grass beside the bowling-green where the gardeners had put up a wild mare for the children — half a tree-trunk lying on its curved edge with a plank fixed across it, so that a child could sit at either end and see-saw up and down. The eldest Kettering boys, Walter and James, were bumping vigorously and thrusting themselves back into the air as the wild mare rolled and creaked. Their sister Elizabeth, a solid girl of seven, was plaintively insisting that it was her turn now.

"Great Eliza wants a ride! D'you hear that, Jamie? She'd never leave the ground."

"I should, I should! And don't call me that name."

"Why, sister — it's one of the names they give to the Queen. There's an ode written for Great Eliza."

Walter winked at James, who added, "It's high treason to speak against the Queen."

Elizabeth burst into tears. She knew

quite well why her brothers tormented her with the nickname, and that it had nothing whatever to do with the Queen.

"Don't cry, sweetheart." John was standing by the wall, idly watching them. He went across to the tree-trunk and told Walter to get off and give Bess a turn.

"Why me, my lord? Why shouldn't it be Jamie?"

"Off."

Walter slid on to the grass, grumbling but not very loud. His parents had observed this foray placidly, Ann merely remarking that John was wonderfully kind to Bess. "It's a pity she's so young."

She had a private daydream about seeing Elizabeth, a few years older (and not nearly so fat) being married to John, in a blaze of triumph.

Her happy reveries were shattered by her husband who said tersely, "If she wasn't so young, I wouldn't have him in the house."

After dinner Kettering had an engagement in the small market town of Gaultonsbury. John went too, and when Bernard and his secretary disappeared into the Mayor's house for a meeting of magistrates, he was left to wander around feeling sorry for himself. It was several years since he had stayed at Minton Gabriel, so he was not known in the district, and the townspeople were quite dazzled by the handsome stranger. From the ruffle of feathers in his hat to his Spanish leather boots, everything about him was exotic and exciting. His discontented expression gave him a certain arrogance, but this rather added to his prestige.

John could not return the compliment. He circled the church twice, surveyed the stocks and the grammar school without interest, and knew that the huddle of narrow grey streets had nothing to offer him.

His walk had brought him once again to the back of the White Swan, the tavern where they had left their horses. He decided he might as well go in. As he sauntered through the stable yard, he was thinking how entertaining life would be if he could meet the sort of girl who would have taken his fancy in London — much hope there was of that in Gaultonsbury.

Then he heard a little eddy of feminine

laughter above his head, looked up, and saw her.

There was an open wooden gallery running along the back of the inn at first-floor level, and two women were leaning on the rail. The one nearest to him was a little red-headed moppet, much too gaudily dressed. He passed her over, it was the other who had captured him instantly: a very striking girl with jet black hair and skin like cream — surely she couldn't be English? French perhaps, or Italian, though what the devil could have brought her to Gaultonsbury? She wore a crimson jacket, and one of those little caps flat on the top of her head; they looked hideous on most people, but not on this impervious beauty who returned his stare with interest, her dark eyes quite unabashed.

Then she spoke, and there was nothing outlandish about her accent. "Will you take care where you tread, sir, I've just dropped an ear-ring; maybe you can see it?"

"Let me have a look — Ah!" John caught sight of something glittering in the dust at his feet. He retrieved the

15

little cluster of quartz, delighted to have this excuse for scraping an acquaintance. "I'll bring it up to you."

He started up the short flight of stairs. The goddesses in the gallery made appropriate sounds of gratitude and pleasure, the red-headed one being particularly effusive. Her dyed hair and her yellow dress reminded him irresistibly of oranges and lemons. There couldn't be much doubt about her state of life; her companion carried things off more successfully, but she was several years younger and much better-looking.

He confronted her on the top step. "Well, I have recovered your treasure; what will you give me in exchange?"

"I'm disappointed in you, sir. I thought you acted from chivalry, and now it turns out you were only out for gain."

"I should be a blind fool otherwise. You would not wish me to be so insensible?"

They were both talking the highly artificial language with which such encounters usually began.

The girl pretended to hesitate. "Perhaps you do deserve some small reward from the owner?"

"That's just what I had in mind."

"Then you shall have your wish," broke in Oranges-and-Lemons, "for I'm very glad to have my ear-ring safe, I wouldn't have lost it for the world."

She advanced on John, almost purring.

He was decidedly put out. "But I thought this belonged to you — " he appealed to the dark girl who, regrettably, was laughing at him.

She began to explain. Her friend, whose name was Margery, had taken the ear-ring off because it pinched.

"And Tamsin was trying to bend the hook when it slipped through her fingers," interrupted Margery. "You can see, I am wearing its fellow."

She was, too. There was nothing for it but to kiss her heartily and wish she was not quite so drenched in scent.

"Easy, my lad. You mustn't take more rewards than you're entitled to." Margery giggled invitingly.

John released her and stood back. He had seen that his dark siren was looking suddenly annoyed, and that rather pleased him. Tamsin. Not the kind of name he would have expected, he wasn't sure whether he liked it.

She had turned to go into a room that led off the gallery, when a man came out and demanded, "How long are you going to lurk out here for? Have you both deserted us?" He broke off on a note of enquiry, as he caught sight of John.

The ear-ring episode was trotted out again, while the two men scrutinised each other. The newcomer was a weathered and worldly individual, with a little pointed beard and a rapier scar on his cheekbone.

He seemed to take kindly to John, for he said, "I'm thankful you found the wretched trinket. Otherwise there would have been an uproar and we should all have been made to hunt for it. Will you come in and drink a cup of sack with us?"

"With great pleasure, sir."

The room they went into was heavy with the reek of wine. Four men were seated round a table, with pewter cups beside them and small heaps of coins. One was shuffling a pack of cards, two were arguing, while the fourth, a stout, elderly Bacchus with a brick-red face,

18

had subsided into his chair and was three parts asleep.

The man with the scar went up to him and shook him by the arm. "Brace yourself, Tom. We have a guest. You must do the honours."

"Tell him . . . go away. No, can't do that . . . hell!" Some dim sense of what was fitting had penetrated the mists of sherris-sack. The stout man raised himself a few inches, blinking towards John with dull solemnity. "Thomas Grove of Sutleigh, at your service. Happy . . . make you welcome."

Grove of Sutleigh, thought John. Lord of the Manor in the next combe to Minton. When he had stayed in these parts before, the Grove in possession had been a learned recluse. He had been succeeded by a disreputable younger brother: John remembered hearing the Ketterings say he was a frequent embarrassment to the surrounding gentry. It was not entirely surprising.

Grove's three cronies were casually identified by the man with the scar, who introduced himself as Toby Strange. There was Gregory Timberlake, a little

19

grey, peevish fellow of about sixty. Matt Webber, a handsome ox who sat astride his stool as though it was a saddle, and looked like a farm boy dressed up for a fair. And at the other extreme, a bony youth called Hannibal Ruskin with a slight nervous tic. They were not an impressive collection.

John raised the cup that Strange had given him, and politely drank their health.

He had not volunteered his own name. No one seemed to mind; old Timberlake was fidgeting, anxious to get on with the game.

Strange glanced at John. "Will you take a hand?"

"You have enough players already."

"Ruskin wants to stand down. And we shan't get much sense out of Grove for the present." Grove had given up the struggle to stay awake; the two women were propping him up and loosening his doublet.

John was in a quandary. He wanted to do anything which would improve his chances of getting on terms with the girl, unluckily he had hardly any money to play with, and Bernard had cut off his allowance.

He said: "I thank you, but I'd prefer to keep out."

The ox-like Webber murmured something about not corrupting innocent babes.

"Would you repeat that?" asked John, his lower lip jutting.

"Why should I repeat it? You can't surely have thought that it had any reference to you?"

John sat down at the table. "I'll play with you," he said.

It was the only thing he could do, with that oaf sneering, and the girl looking on. He didn't feel very confident. He had met men like Strange before, and suspected that he was one of those coney-catchers who made a living at cards. The game was trump, where skill counted as much as luck.

Timberlake cut the deck and began to deal. John picked up a hand which seemed to consist entirely of deuces and treys. Glancing across the room in a preoccupied way, he found Tamsin watching him. She gave him an entrancing smile, and came round to stand behind him. Encouraged, he laid down his first card. To start with, it was a simple matter of following suit; then there came a moment of decision. As he paused, she leant over and tweaked out the right card.

"Let me tell you something, Tamsin," said Strange, quite pleasantly.

"Well, Toby?"

"The rules of war allow no mercy for spies."

It was only then that John realised she had been able to see into both their hands. He immediately offered to forfeit his advantage. Tamsin laughed and told him not to be softhearted, but she did not intervene again.

In fact, John was comfortably holding his own; he soon got the idea that Strange was letting him win on purpose to draw him on.

He didn't really want to spend an April afternoon shut up in the stuffy private room of a tavern, poring over the cards till they made him squint. The little group he had got into looked as though they were inured to such surroundings: the sot and the gambler, their dubious hangers-on, and the pair of doxies. He wondered which of the men Tamsin belonged to; he was afraid it was Strange. It would be much harder to take her away from him than from any of the others.

He tried to sound her. "You haven't always lived here."

"Is that a question or a statement?"

"Put it down to justifiable curiosity."

"The game, man — the game!" snorted Gregory Timberlake.

John absentmindedly threw away his best card by mistake. After that he decided he would have to concentrate, and he did not hear the new arrival who presently came in, until a drawling voice said: "What an edifying spectacle."

The voice was so familiar to John that he spun round guiltily. But all was well; his cousin's secretary was alone, there was no sign of Bernard.

Edmund Royden hailed several of the party, whom he seemed to know, but spoke directly to John.

"I thought your lordship might care to learn that Sir Bernard has finished his business with the Mayor."

"In that case I must finish mine."

John threw down the last card in his hand with an assumed nonchalance; at least he could escape from this intolerable game. He had just made an interesting discovery. When Royden came out with his title, he happened to be looking at Strange, and it was quite clearly no news to him. So he'd been deliberately angling all along. And the girl?

He had no chance to look at her, for Mr. Gregory Timberlake had now taken the field.

"What's this — his lordship? What lordship? Why wasn't I told? If it is indeed Sir Bernard's cousin, you'd think I should have been the first person — my dear lord, forgive me, I am out of touch with the world: so long since I came to the Court. But I should have recognised you, I feel sure you must be the grandson of my old friend."

"I'm Harcourt de Laleham," said John bleakly.

"I wish I'd known it earlier," remarked Margery.

She'd probably have kissed him twice as hard. He couldn't help rather liking

24

Margery, and anything was better than this sycophant Timberlake, with his mixture of fawning and familiarity, and his fictitious anecdotes about John's grandfather. He made it impossible to attend to anyone else, and in the final hurry John had to leave without exchanging another word with Tamsin.

Outside on the gallery stair, he asked Royden: "How did you know I was there?"

"The ostler told me. I thought your lordship would be glad of a warning, but I'm sorry I was so clumsy about it. I didn't know you were incognito."

"I don't think I was; I'm sure Strange had recognised me. Edmund, what do you know of the girl? Which of those men is her protector?"

"Margery? She's Tom Grove's little lightskirt; he's not always so drunk as he appeared this afternoon."

"Not Margery — Tamsin. You can't tell me she is Grove's mistress also."

"No, she's his daughter."

"His *daughter* — Good God!" John came to a standstill, thunderstruck. "What is she doing in that den of iniquity? Even if her father's too depraved to care, you'd think the rest of the family would have some say — "

"Tamsin has no family, in the sense you mean, my lord. She's not legitimate."

"Oh, his bastard!"

John was relieved. For a moment he had been appalled by the errors and blunders he seemed to have been making in the past two hours, but now that he knew the truth, he could imagine why Tamsin fitted so snugly into her setting. She must have inherited tastes from both sides — and she had probably inherited nothing else, unless her looks came from her mother. It would have been no one's duty to waste time and energy restraining her from a life which obviously suited her so well.

★ ★ ★

In the room behind the gallery Tamsin was asking Toby Strange, "Did you know who he was all the time?"

"Certainly I knew. I've watched him swaggering about London these past three months with a king's ransom on his back;

I never dreamed I'd get so close to him as I did today. And what must you do, my sweet fool, but go setting up as his champion, and cramping my style so that you spoilt everything. What came over you?"

"He seemed so reluctant. I wondered if he hadn't enough money to stake with. I see now I must have been wrong; is he very rich?"

"So rich that he makes Kettering look threadbare. Still, there's no harm done. We've whetted his appetite; we'll soon get him over to Sutleigh."

"But not to play cards," said Margery. "There's only one game that young man cares about, and he'll want Tamsin for a partner. My dear, I'm green with envy. If I were you, I should be running home to put clean sheets on the bed."

Tamsin laughed. "You could hardly do less for a lord."

"And *you* need hardly do so much," said Strange in a low voice. "Tamsin, how well did you like him?"

She did not answer, because one of the inn servants came in just then, and asked rather disdainfully if they were keeping the room any longer.

"For another hour at least," said Gregory Timberlake, casting an experienced eye over his old friend Tom Grove who was still sleeping off his orgy. "You'd better bring us some supper. And another flagon of wine."

By the time they had eaten, Tom Grove's brain had cleared enough for them to rouse him and plant him on his horse. Matt Webber went off to his own house on the edge of the town, and the rest of the party set out for Sutleigh. They followed a rutty track across the moor, until they came to a place where it forked left and right into the neighbouring valleys of Sutleigh and Minton, which stretched side by side with a steep ridge between them.

They bore left. The Manor of Sutleigh was quite near the mouth of the combe: a squat stone building, improved and enlarged in King Henry's reign, and neglected ever since. It was a long time since anyone had clipped the yew hedge which looked as rough and ill-kempt as the coat of a moorland pony. There was grass sprouting between the flagstones in

28

the courtyard, and half the stable block was falling down because Mr. Grove had found it convenient to sell the lead off the roof. Tamsin was always conscious of these things, but she did not dwell on them this evening. She hurried into the house, leaving the others to deal with her father.

Matters were a little better indoors; she had done what she could. The furniture was vigorously polished, and the rushes on the floor changed once a fortnight. No amount of patching and hard work could restore the dingy tapestries that were hanging apart from sheer old age; between their gaping shreds you could glimpse the beamed walls, like the bones of the houses beneath the flesh. For some reason she found herself remembering the light, high elegant rooms at Minton Gabriel, and the pretty painted ceilings she had admired so much the only time she had ever been asked inside.

Her father's old manservant had come with a taper to light the hall candles.

"Where's Master Simon?" she enquired.

"Eating his supper, Mrs. Tamsin."

She found him in the parlour — a

big, awkward headlong boy with untidy hair and brilliant hazel eyes. He was her fourteen-year-old half-brother; they were both illegitimate.

Simon wagged his knife at her and went on munching pigeon pie.

"I'm glad to see you are not starving," she said. "I wanted to get home earlier, but I see there was no need. How went the day at school?"

"The same as ever. Old Grizzly-guts was after my blood. How I hate the place! Why do I have to stay there?"

"Because my father wishes you to be a gentleman."

"Oh, fiddle! He doesn't care what becomes of me. He'd soon let me leave school if you would but change his mind for him. Tamsin, why won't you?"

"I want you to escape, get away from Sutleigh; you won't do that unless you are properly educated."

"What I need is money, and we never have any."

"Money alone isn't enough, Simon. That's what I keep trying to tell you. Think of poor Matt Webster, a miser's son brought up like a ploughboy. What use can Matt make of his wealth now he's got it?"

"He has some splendid horses; I wouldn't mind being in Matt's shoes. Would you rather I took after Toby? He's clever enough to set the Thames on fire."

Tamsin frowned. It was true that Toby Strange, living on his wits and other people's folly, was an example of what might happen to an intelligent man who found the more respectable careers shut to him through poverty and lack of influence. The truth was that you had to have both education and money — what sort of an outlook was that for Simon?

She perched on the edge of the table, swinging one foot and contemplating her half-brother. She was very fond of him. They were completely unalike; Tamsin was the image of her mother, the beautiful Julian Trelawney who had fallen fatally in love with young Tom Grove before he was bloated by lassitude and drink. She had run away from her husband, he had deserted his wife, and they had lived a wandering, precarious and scandal-ridden life together for ten years until she died.

31

Grove had been kind, within his limits, and loyal; he hadn't been faithful. One of his fancies was a tavern-keeper's daughter in Holborn, with no more morals than the tavern cat. She had a child, swore Tom Grove had fathered it, and abandoned it dramatically on his doorstep. Grove was too soft-hearted to hand over the little creature to the constable, but he didn't really believe he was the father, so Simon was hustled into the background and dragged up among the servants. Tamsin, of course, had always been acknowledged, and treated exactly as though her parents were married.

Unexpectedly, it was Tamsin who adored Simon. From the time that she was four and he was a tiny baby, she wanted to have him as her real brother and an equal. It took her ten years to get her way, more or less. By then her mother was dead, and her father had brought his ramshackle entourage down to Sutleigh, where he had just inherited the family estate. He was feeling vaguely patriarchal, and several of his friends had begun to point out that the little boy Simon was an unmistakeable Grove;

whatever his mother might have been, there couldn't be much doubt that Tom was his father.

Tamsin was delighted. Simon, once he had discovered the consequences, was not. He had been living almost entirely in the stables; now he was made to wash and dress up and mind his manners, and sent off daily to Gaultonsbury Grammar School, where his father hoped he would be flogged into the proper amount of learning. And even Tamsin nagged.

"If you could get to a University," she said, now.

"I doubt I'm too stupid."

"I doubt you're too lazy. The trouble is, you've no ambition, no idea what a much better life you might have, among men who are so different from — oh well, never mind!" Tamsin reached over and helped herself to a comfit which she popped in her mouth. "You'll never guess who we met in Gaultonsbury. Sir Bernard Kettering's cousin, the young lord."

"What was he like then? Very proud and haughty?"

"No, he was exceedingly gallant.

Margery was all of a twitter."

"Perhaps he'll take her off our hands."

"Poor Margery, that's unkind of you. We might fare worse. At least she doesn't fly into rages and box your ears. Or weep all day long because it rains so much in the country."

"Or complain about the dogs."

They both laughed, remembering some of their father's former mistresses.

And anyway, that young man wanted me, not Margery, thought Tamsin, but she did not say this aloud. At fourteen, Simon had still not fully realised the ambiguities of her position.

★ ★ ★

At about the same time, two miles across the hill, Ann Kettering was saying to her husband, "I asked Charity and Michael to wait on us after supper; there are so many matters to discuss."

They were in her small withdrawing-room, which led out of the long gallery. Bernard was sitting at one end of a cushioned day bed, leaning back with the air of a man who had finished a hard day and was enjoying a spell of peace and silence. He shut his eyes and said nothing.

"We have to talk about the wedding." Ann sounded a little defensive.

"Do we? You and Charity may feel obliged to talk about it; I fancy Michael and I will simply agree with every word you say — if we know what's best for us."

She laughed. "To be sure, you are very ill-used. John, I hope you aren't taken in by his browbeaten aspect."

"Not in the least, madam," said John cheerfully. He stood up. "Would you like me to go? Since you have private matters to discuss?"

But they assured him that there was nothing private about the arrangements for the wedding of Michael Rivers and Charity Mulcaster; no one at Minton could think about anything else.

The bride was one of Lady Kettering's waiting-gentlewomen; her parents lived over the hill in the parish of Sutleigh, where the marriage would take place next week. The bridegroom came from the other end of the county; working in Sir Bernard's household, and being trained by his steward, was a kind of apprenticeship to fit him for managing his own property later on.

The betrothed couple came in together. Michael Rivers was a tough young man with a blunt, humorous face; Charity was a small, appealing girl, her eyes as soft and grave as a doe's. They were rather tongue-tied at first, but were soon induced to talk on the irresistible subject of their wedding. John had withdrawn slightly from the group and was reading a book called *The Discoverie of Witchcraft* which he had picked up in his cousin's library. Along with all the accounts of weird ritual and horrid practices, he could not help absorbing a good deal of very dull information about the wedding.

"Who are your bridesmaids?" asked Ann presently. "Your sister, of course, and Agnes. Who else?"

"Catherine Maltby, madam, and my Wilshaw cousins from Garth. And Tamsin. Tamsin Grove."

"Tamsin *Grove*?" repeated Ann, on a rising inflexion.

John sat up with a jerk and nearly

dropped his book. He saw the Ketterings exchange glances; he was quite as astonished as they were.

Charity said: "I am very fond of Tamsin, my lady. I always have been, ever since she first came to the combe, four years ago."

"Yes, I know how kind your mother was to her then. All the same — "

"It isn't Tamsin's fault that her parents weren't married," persisted Charity, pink and ridiculously fierce; a pretty little doe at bay, John decided.

"It may not be her fault, but it has led to some very unfortunate consequences. And your mother is so good and unworldly, it might not occur to her to wonder what Mr. and Mrs. Rivers may think when they find a girl of Tamsin's reputation among the bridesmaids."

Michael started to say that his parents wouldn't care a fig for the bridesmaids' reputations; realised that this wasn't going to help, and stuck.

It was Kettering's calm voice which threw a bridge across the chasm of awkwardness that was beginning to widen. "I've no doubt Michael's parents will accept the bridesmaids without question. Certainly no one else has the right to cavil."

His wife started to speak, but thought better of it. After a brief pause, the conversation sprang up again, though not quite so easily as before.

John pretended to read his book, ears pricked now, for every mention of the wedding, which might not be such a tedious affair after all, if that siren was going to grace the proceedings. He had been wondering all the evening how to find out more about her without making Bernard suspicious. That problem at least had been solved.

Presently Michael and Charity said good night, and directly the door closed behind them the Ketterings began a violent argument.

"No right to cavil! Have you gone mad, Bernard? You know very well what sort of a girl she is, living in that den of iniquity, and brazening it around the countryside with all those men — "

"She lives in her father's house and associates with his friends; you can't describe that as a deadly sin, and there is nothing else proved against her."

"That's not how you generally speak of her. You think she's a wanton, and you can't deny it."

"Ann, do try to understand that what you and I think privately is neither here nor there. If that young woman had lived openly with a lover, or had a child, or been disgraced by some notorious scandal, you might refuse to meet her. As it is, you can't possibly do so without insulting the Mulcasters."

Ann had got up and was fidgeting with the ornaments on the top of the court-cupboard. He went to stand beside her.

"Come, my dear. It's not like you to be unkind. Tamsin had a wretched upbringing, she isn't entirely to blame for what she has become."

"I'm not condemning her. I wouldn't mind meeting her anywhere else, only she ought not to be a bridesmaid. It's very wrong."

"Well, if it's merely a question of her lost virginity," said Bernard drily, "you had better go to London and tell the Queen you object to half her Maids of Honour for the same reason."

"Oh, you men are all alike!" Ann flung up her head with a sudden anger. "You don't care what a woman does, provided she's handsome enough. You treat everything as a matter for levity."

She turned and ran out of the room, slamming the door.

Bernard took one step after her, hesitated, and stayed where he was. He had caught sight of John.

Their eyes met, just as John realised his lapse of good manners. He shouldn't be gaping here; he ought to have left the room directly his cousins started quarrelling. He began to apologise.

"I beg your pardon, Sir. I had no business to remain, but the truth is, I was taken by surprise."

"So was I," rejoined Bernard a little ruefully. "It was my own fault. Trying to excuse one woman to another is like lighting a candle on a hay-rick."

He would have to go and comfort Ann, who was probably sobbing her heart out by now. With a mixture of love and irritation, he felt obliged to defend her to John.

"True virtue is its own safeguard. Ann

is so armed against temptation that the weakness of other women seems to her incomprehensible, monstrous . . . Well, I would not have her otherwise."

John murmured something acquiescent. He quite understood Bernard's attitude. When he eventually got married himself, he would require his wife to be as innocent and faithful as Ann. In the meantime, those other women were a good deal more entertaining.

★ ★ ★

"Have you a dress fit for the occasion?" Tom Grove asked his daughter.

It was rather late to start worrying about Tamsin's dress, two hours before the wedding. But that was typical of Grove. He himself was in breeches and shirtsleeves, seated at a table in the big bedchamber he shared, at present, with the red-headed Margery. The combined efforts of his mistress and his daughter had got him to bed sober the night before, his servant had just shaved him, and now he was breakfasting on bread and beef and beer.

41

"Never mind me," said Tamsin. "The question is, what are *you* going to wear? You've torn a rent in the sleeve of your black doublet, and you've nothing else sufficiently fine."

"He can't wear the blue," Margery pointed out. "He's grown too fat for it."

"I won't be seen dead with him in the blue. I think I can mend this so it will be hidden by the braid. Have you a needle and thread, Margery? No matter, I'll fetch one."

As she went out of the room, her father asked rather anxiously, "What does she intend to wear, do you know?"

It dawned on him that bridesmaids generally had garments which were not at all like Tamsin's usual wardrobe.

"She got what she wanted, made to order in Gaultonsbury."

He hoped that was all right; it was a pity that his motherless child should have grown up with no one to advise her but his doxies; splendid creatures, of course, but they didn't really know much about the manners and deportment of young gentlewomen. He should have provided Tamsin with a stepmother, but how could he, when his original, long-deserted wife insisted on staying alive, purely to spite him?

"I hear you're appearing in gorgeous new apparel," he said when Tamsin returned with his doublet, invisibly repaired. And as an afterthought, "Who's going to pay for it?"

"You are. Why? Did you think I might ask Toby?"

Grove preferred to let the subject drop. So far he had managed not to find out the exact truth about his eighteen-year-old daughter's relations with the soldier of fortune and professional gambler, Toby Strange. He was afraid it might make him feel ashamed, and this uncomfortable experience must be avoided at all costs. He was thankful when she left him to finish dressing.

Twenty minutes later she sailed in again all in pale yellow, her neck and shoulders clouded by a gauze cape which fell from the tiny frilled ruff at her throat; her body was sheathed in thick, heavy silk that leapt into a wide arc at the farthingale, swinging at every move. The skirt was divided down the front, and parted to reveal a petticoat embroidered with tiny flowers. Her long hair hung down her back, brushed to a sculptured smoothness and invincibly black. Her face was rather pale.

Margery exclaimed, "Why, you look like a bride yourself!"

"Handsomer than most," said Grove, relieved to find that Tamsin was dressed exactly as she ought to be.

"I wish I could be there to see you in all your glory." The brassy little courtesan sounded almost wistful.

"It will be no triumphal progress," Tamsin assured her. "I shall be a fish out of water in that worshipful assembly, and I'm frightened to death."

Margery might not believe her, but it was more than half true. She could be sure of finding some friendliness among their neighbours, people who would be casually kind, plenty of men to admire her. For these reasons, it was worth braving a few snubs to go out in company whenever she got the chance. But being a bridesmaid at a wedding, that was different. She would be at the mercy of the other women — the league of well-dowered, legitimately born, sheltered ladies of irreproachable reputation; she thought they would probably tear her in pieces.

Riding pillion behind her father, she shivered inside the cloak that was protecting her from the dust. They had not far to go; just the length of the village and its three huge fields that were shared between the whole community. The first one had already been sown with rye last autumn, and the second would lie fallow all this year. The men had started to fence the third field for the spring sowing: oats, beans and vetches. Not that anyone was working this morning. It was a holiday, because of the wedding.

They came to the village green, with the church on the right, and the big house, Abbotsleat, on the left. They dismounted at the stone gateway, their horse was led away to the stables; Grove gave his daughter an encouraging pat, and went across on foot to join the congregation in the church.

Tamsin was left alone to meet her fate.

A serving-man escorted her up the short, flagged path and into the house. The bridesmaids were waiting in a room at the back, with several older women fussing over them. The first person she saw was Lady Kettering, who inspected her coldly, and said, "We thought you were going to be late."

Tamsin curtsied, merely saying she was sorry — and then thought scornfully, why the devil did I do that? I'm not late, so there's nothing to be sorry about.

She faced the four girls who were avidly studying her. Honor Mulcaster, the bride's sister, was upstairs helping her to dress. Down here were their cousins Isobel and Phoebe Wilshaw, the pretty and rather spoilt Kate Maltby, and Agnes Morton who, like Charity, was one of Lady Kettering's waiting-gentlewomen. By agreement, they were all dressed in yellow, a colour with a symbolism that was suitable for weddings.

"I see I've come in the right livery," said Tamsin, more or less at random, to Phoebe Wilshaw.

The answer was a dumb stare.

Self-righteous cow, thought Tamsin. It

did not occur to her that Phoebe was merely over-awed. The young Wilshaws, having been warned against Tamsin by their mother, naturally regarded her as a creature of the most enviable guile and wickedness.

Two small boys were also watching her: James and Walter Kettering, scrubbed within an inch of their lives and wearing bright-coloured favours on their sleeves.

"We have to take the bride to church," James informed Tamsin importantly.

"Have you indeed? I hope you won't lose your way."

The two boys were overcome by this witticism. They hooted with glee, and their mother looked suspicious.

Heaven help me, thought Tamsin satirically, what a desperate harpy I must be. No man is safe from my snares.

She was glad when it was time to conduct the bridegroom to church.

Michael had ridden over from Minton with several of his family to support him. His blue doublet and hose were trimmed with silver lace. He looked nervous but determined.

As the bridesmaids came out of the house to meet him, they were each handed a basket of primroses. They formed up in pairs and walked ahead of him, strewing his path with flowers.

All the villagers were there to see the six fair maids, fresh as a garland of daffodils, leading the fine young gentleman to his wedding.

"Like a lamb to the slaughter," observed one cynic in the crowd. His wife told him sharply to hold his tongue.

As soon as they had delivered Michael to the church door, the girls went back across their trodden primroses to fetch the bride, who was just emerging from the house. She was dressed in a milk-white gown, with true-lover's-knots in russet and pale blue stitched on her skirt, and like her bridesmaids, she wore her long hair down over her shoulders, the traditional sign of virginity. Her two young groomsmen, James and Walter, stood gravely, one each side of her.

They processed across the green, under the Norman arch, and into the parish church. When they came in, the air was filled with the soft whisper of silks, the click of swords in their scabbards, as the congregation turned expectantly towards them. Gliding up the aisle with infinite dignity, they came to rest by the front pew, and Tamsin found herself nearly standing on the brass memorial of Sir Richard Grove, a hero of Agincourt. She was surrounded by her dead ancestors, whose name she had no legal right to use.

The vicar began to read the marriage service. " . . . gathered together here in the sight of God, and in the face of this congregation . . . join together this man and this woman . . . an honourable estate . . . time of man's innocency . . . Cana of Galilee . . . taken in hand . . . reverently, discreetly, advisedly, soberly, and in the fear of God; duly considering the causes for which Matrimony was ordained . . . "

Terrible and overwhelming phrases, thought Tamsin, for whom they always had a somewhat bitter flavour. Michael and Charity seemed totally enraptured. The service went on: the questions, vows and prayers. So far everything had been as reverent, discreet and sober as you could wish, but suddenly the mood was changed, splintered like a pane of breaking glass. As the newly-married couple rose to their feet after the blessing, there was an automatic stir throughout the church, and all the young bachelors came pouring out of the pews and up the aisle, surrounding the bride, pulling the true-lover's-knots off her skirt and scrambling for her garters.

Charity squeaked and protested, clinging to Michael, who was doing his best to defend her from their enthusiastic friends, while in some danger of having the points of his own doublet torn off as well.

"Go easy, you clowns! Can't you leave us a rag to our backs?"

But he was laughing really, and so was she. This was all part of the ordeal, and they had known it would happen. It always happened.

The young blades were sticking the knots of ribbon in their hats; the two who had captured the bride's garters were each demanding the customary pair of gloves; the cup of muscadel was being handed round with a tray of little cakes, and various members of the bridal families were embracing. And of course the bachelors had started to kiss the bridesmaids.

Tamsin was seized from behind by a pair of remarkably strong hands, and twirled round to face a tall young man she didn't immediately recognise as he stooped to kiss her mouth. Tilting her head back, she was able to focus on a pair of very dark blue eyes that were laughing into her own, and a well-remembered voice said, "This is what I wanted to do the first time we met."

"You can't have expected to do it here, my lord."

"Why else do you think I came to this marriage — my sacred and profane love?"

The last words were said very low; they should not have been spoken at all in this place. Kissing at weddings was all very well, but no one ought to feel in church the treacherous quickening of the blood she felt in the proximity of this much too handsome young man.

She disengaged herself as smoothly as possible and was greeted by Edmund Royden, Kettering's secretary, who had always admired her without wanting

51

to do anything else. She noticed that Lord Harcourt was embracing the other bridesmaids with complete impartiality.

At the wedding breakfast they were seated a short way apart on opposite sides of the table. John was in the place of honour next to the bride and groom. Tamsin, as a bridesmaid, was placed much higher than she would have been otherwise. They were not close enough to talk, but they were each physically overwhelmed by the other's presence. John knew just what had happened when he kissed her, for at nineteen he was already experienced enough to recognise the faintest quiver of a response, however soon it was checked. So they were both after the same thing, and as far as he could see there was no obstacle — apart from a certain degree of caution and good manners — to stop them.

Towards the end of the meal, Mr. Mulcaster said to his daughter, "Old Salathiel is outside, do you want to have him in?"

"Yes, to be sure. He promised he'd be at my wedding."

"Who is Salathiel?" asked John.

"A ballad-singer, my lord, and very well known in these parts. He comes to all the feasts."

Michael said, "Charity wouldn't feel we were properly married unless Salathiel was here. "

Salathiel was brought in and paid his respects to the company, most of whom he seemed to know personally. He was a lean old fellow with a ragged beard, not in the least like the spruce ballad-singers who flourished around London, selling printed broadsheets about the latest Tyburn hanging. Salathiel had no broadsheets, and probably could not read. No one knew where his songs came from, and no one had written them down; he carried them in his head, from village to village, and they spread across the countryside like thistledown.

He scraped a chord on his fiddle and lifted an old voice that was dry but still sweet, like the taste of a russet apple.

"Abroad as I was walking, down by
    yon green woodside,
I heard a young girl singing, 'I wish
    I were a bride'.

'I thank you, pretty fair maid, for
   singing of your song;
Tis I myself will marry you.' 'Kind
   sir, I am too young.'

'The younger the better, more fitting
   for a bride,
That all the world may plainly see I
   won a pretty maid.'

Nine times I kissed her ruby lips, I
   viewed her sparkling eye,
I took her by her lily-white hand, my
   lovely bride-to-be."

Everyone smiled and approved. Salathiel
sang two more songs, and by that time
even the most gluttonous guests had
finished eating and drinking. The trestles
were removed and the dancing began.

Tamsin was never short of partners.
Presently she was dancing with a pleasant
young man called Giles Brown whom she
had not met before; he was staying at
Minton Gabriel.

"You're a friend of the bridegroom?"

"No. Well, that's a churlish thing to
say, isn't it? I like him very well, but I

didn't know him until I came to Minton with my master a fortnight ago."

"Do you mean Lord Harcourt de Laleham? Is he your master?"

"Yes."

"Have you been long in his service?"

"Ten years. Does that surprise you? I entered his lordship's household on my ninth birthday; we are much of an age, and my father was his steward. We shared the same tutor, and later I went with him to Oxford."

She went on asking questions. Giles Brown seemed to be much attached to Lord Harcourt, and it interested her to hear more about the young nobleman whose life was so remote from anything she could imagine. When he came of age and kept a proper state at Crossingbourne, she gathered, he would employ three hundred servants, and he would hardly be able to dress himself or open a door unaided. While he was living privately in his guardian's house, there were no more than eight human beings with the sole duty of caring for his needs — and four of them were in charge of his horses.

"Paltry," said Tamsin. "What a life of hardship you must all be leading."

They had been walking through a rather leisurely pavane; when the music stopped, he took her to sit on a bench against the wall. "Tell me more about Lord Harcourt," she encouraged him. "Your whole account sounds like a fairytale to me."

"Will you let Lord Harcourt tell you himself?" said a voice at her elbow.

Tamsin was very seldom put out of countenance, but she did feel slightly annoyed that Harcourt should have caught her fishing for gossip from one of his servants. He was gazing down at her from his magnificent height with an amusement she did not altogether trust.

Rallying, she said: "You had far better let Mr. Brown go on singing your praises, my lord. Unless you are a very good trumpeter."

"Has he done me justice?" Harcourt glanced at his henchman, who had got to his feet. "My dear Giles, I am grateful. Now you may remove yourself and dance with some of those worthy, tedious young women on the other side of the hill. I am going to claim a monopoly of Mrs. Tamsin Grove."

"Very well, my lord," said Giles Brown, who was apparently used to his master's unquestioning egotism. He bowed and moved away.

Tamsin was not used to it, and was preparing to say so, when Robin Mulcaster, the bride's brother, clapped his hands and announced: "My lord — ladies — gentlemen! There'll be no more dancing for the present. We're going to play hide-and-seek."

Some of the party were pleased, some were not.

"These country weddings!" grumbled Kate Maltby, who had once been to Court and never let anyone forget it. "Your lordship will find little to satisfy you in such rustic fooling."

"On the contrary, madam. I suggested it."

I might have known, thought Tamsin as she joined the circle of young people who were all arguing about the rules and which rooms were to be used. She could see that she was going to be engaged in another sort of game, or perhaps you might call it a fencing match.

John Harcourt was next to her when they all trailed out of the hall and began choosing places to hide. Safety in numbers, thought Tamsin, attaching herself to a fairly large group that was headed by Robin Mulcaster and his cousin Isobel Wilshaw. They decided to go upstairs. It was extraordinary how many people the low, rather dark rooms could absorb, if they squeezed close enough, and stayed still enough to melt into the furniture. They were disappearing, with many shoves and giggles, under beds and under tables, behind doors and inside closets and within the folds of the arras. Charity and Michael had got on top of the linen press and covered themselves with a quilt.

"I heard a story once," whispered one of the girls, "of a wedding where they played hide-and-seek, and the bride got into a chest, and the lid came down on her and she couldn't get out. She was never seen again. Not for years and years, until they opened the chest, and discovered a skeleton in a bridal wreath!"

She shivered deliciously.

"They must have had very poor noses," said Isobel. "Or they'd have smelt her out as soon as she started stinking. Robin, let's go up to the attics."

"Shall you and I try our luck here?" suggested John to Tamsin, driving her dexterously towards one of the bedchambers.

"I think not, my lord."

Tamsin hurried after the main party. Several of the others had wandered off, but she was able to follow Isobel and Robin up the steep steps into the attic. They reached a long, narrow chamber where the maidservants slept at night on straw mattresses. Tamsin walked the length of this gallery with John at her heels: she had caught a glimpse of Isobel going into a little screened alcove at one corner.

Tamsin rounded the screen and stopped dead. Isobel and Robin were two feet away, clasped in the throes of a most abandoned embrace. They were not at all glad to see her.

"Oh!" said Tamsin.

She retreated, straight into John

Harcourt, who was grinning in a most irritating way.

"I thought you were being somewhat indiscreet."

"Well, how was I to know?"

"My poor girl, you must be blind. They've been mooning after each other all day."

Because he was blocking the way back to the stairs, she went on into a further attic, which was stacked with broken stools and leather cloak-bags, and rolls of old, moth-eaten tapestry, the usual clutter that no one could ever bring themselves to throw away. John came after her. They were now bound to have the scene which had, in any case, become inevitable. The sooner the better, and if she couldn't handle this boy she must be greener than she had any right to be.

She turned round. It was very quiet; far down in the house they could hear the faint cry of the players: "All hid! All hid!"

"Sweetheart, I thought we should never contrive to be alone. Stand still, my pet. You are so beautiful, I want to eat you with my eyes first, and after that — "

"My dear lord, I am not your sweetheart or your pet — "

"You soon will be," he said, frustrating her efforts to slide out of his grasp. "My treasure, you have the most enchanting mouth — "

"It's of no use trying to cozen me with honeyed words — and take your hands off me, you impudent lout!" flashed Tamsin on a sudden change of key.

She had felt the keen edge of his teeth against her lips, followed by some extremely predatory tactics that she was not going to tolerate for one second.

She kicked him sharply on the ankle, and trod on his foot as heavily as she could manage. He gave a gasp of pain and let her go. Not so much a fencing match as a wrestling match, she thought, hitching up the rim of her bodice.

He smiled at her, rather ruefully, and rubbed his instep. "What a vixen you are. I'm sorry if I acted too impatiently." It was the merest shadow of an apology. "I thought you were as hot for it as I am."

"You flatter yourself, my lord."

"Do I? Then why did you come up

here with me, what else did you expect?"
He gave her no chance to reply. "You
knew how it was between us at the
first instant of our first meeting. You
are perfectly aware that I want to lie
with you, so why waste time pretending
otherwise?"

She surveyed him as he leant against
an old wicker hamper, lazily confident.
He was flushed from the excitements of
the last few minutes, and a lock of dark
hair drifted across his forehead.

She said, as distinctly as possible: "I
am not pretending anything, my lord.
I am refusing. Or I should be, if your
lordship had ever had the courtesy to ask
for my consent."

He was astounded. "Refusing?" he
repeated. "But why? Why should you
refuse? I thought you liked me."

"Poor Lord Harcourt, I dare say you
never met with a setback until now?"

John did not answer. He was angry and
mystified. She was making him sound
a complete coxcomb, and it was quite
unjust. Naturally he did not imagine that
every woman he met would fall at his
feet. But like many rich young men in

search of amusement, he considered it wiser to deal with the sort of women who were known to be accessible, and since he had a great deal to recommend him he had never before found himself courting a mistress who did not receive him with enthusiasm. Besides, he had been so sure that she found him attractive; what motive could she have for refusing?

"Are you in love?" he demanded. "With Toby Strange?"

"What would you do if I was?"

"Retire gracefully, I suppose."

He had no wish to compete against anyone else's tragic attitudes and heart-searing passions. It was easy come, easy go, for him.

"I dare say you would prefer me to be in love," she remarked. "It would appease your wounded vanity."

John's vanity was still practically unscathed.

"Come, Tamsin," he said, "don't plague me any more. I don't know what I've done to offend you — "

"And I doubt if you'll ever guess."

"You might at least — What's that? Listen."

There were footsteps approaching, and noisy whoops and calls, as the searchers in the game of hide-and-seek arrived on the top floor to flush their quarry. So strong was the atavistic fear of the hunted, that John and Tamsin forgot their differences and stood like statues inside their concealing bastion of rubbish.

They heard Robin and Isobel being detected with a good deal of lewd merriment.

Robin was being recalcitrant. "A pox on you all for a set of killjoys. Can't you let us be?"

"No, we need some prisoners to show for our labours. Is there anyone else up here?"

"Tamsin and Lord Harcourt came up after us," said Isobel. "But they went away again."

"What's Tamsin doing with that popinjay?" It was one of her local swains, slightly the worse for drink. "I'll set him to rights, I'll crack his jaw for him, I swear I will."

His friends thought this very funny, and started making dire prophecies about what would happen if he did.

"He'll have you indicted for treason."

"Cast into a dungeon."

"Interfering with the pastimes of the nobility; that's bound to be a felony. Or a misdemeanour."

"I should let Harcourt commit his own misdemeanours, he looks very well able to."

Tamsin could not resist making a grimace at her companion, who winked at her. It was obvious that if they were found at this juncture, everyone was going to be embarrassed, so they stayed where they were, hoping for the best, and after a desultory hunt in the outer attic, the pursuers went away again.

"You see what sort of a character you bear," said Tamsin.

"Yes, a veritable tyrant. I wonder you didn't scream to be rescued."

"I was afraid you might cast me into a dungeon."

"I wish I had the power. Not that I'd do it. I'd sooner carry you off into the woods — "

" 'To hear the fond tale of the sweet nightingale, as she sings in the valleys below'?"

65

He smiled at the quotation, a rather wry smile, for of course he knew this song, and a good many other seduction-songs, each of them using a different and delightful poetic fancy with which to suggest the same crude transaction — a carnal and temporary enjoyment that was not going to be rarefied or elevated into something better by a few heady verses about nightingales.

Well, he had recognised that at the outset. He had paid her the compliment of approaching her honestly, without a lot of play-acting. And that hadn't suited her either. So what did she want, this difficult, beautiful girl?

He said: "Don't be unkind to me. I long so much to love you. Only tell me what price I have to pay?"

"Is your lordship offering me money to go to bed with you?"

"I shouldn't dream of it," said John hastily.

He was quite prepared to offer her money if she asked for it (regardless of the fact that at present he had not got any.) But now, at last, he thought he knew what was wrong. Meeting her at the White Swan with Margery, he had misjudged Tamsin's exact status, and possibly she had guessed and felt insulted. Since then he had decided that Tom Grove's daughter was certainly not a harlot, but one of those independent wantons who did for pleasure — and often with a careless generosity — what other women did for gain. He had noticed that these ladies did not mind collecting some fairly valuable presents, and the sin was the same in either case, but they were inclined to be curiously touchy.

He did his best to soothe any feelings he might have ruffled. "When I spoke of paying a price, I meant metaphorically; I know you would not come to me except of your own choice. We are free spirits, after all."

"If I were you, my lord, I should leave our spirits out of it. Your sole concern is with our bodies."

A palpable hit, he thought, staring at her through the gloom: by now the sun had set, and not much light seeped in through the little dormer window with its curtain of cobwebs. In this grey limbo, Tamsin had not lost any of her lustre;

she had acquired a hint of aloofness and mystery to counter-balance the mockery, and the warm flesh and blood. He had never seen a girl he desired so much.

She said, "We ought not to stay here any longer," and when he protested, she pointed out that the game of hide-and-seek was probably over, and they would soon be missed.

John was reminded that his guardian would be on the watch for him; the last thing he wanted was trouble with Bernard. It would be more sensible to call off the siege for this evening, and escort Tamsin downstairs to join the other guests. The wedding festivities had four more days to go.

★ ★ ★

As it turned out, John had no more solitary conversations with Tamsin at Abbotsleat. She did not avoid him, in fact they danced together several times, but as there were no other games of hide-and-seek, they were continually surrounded by people, with no excuse to wander away on their own.

He managed a surreptitious visit to the Manor the following week. This was a disastrous evening — he never saw Tamsin alone, and lost a good deal of money playing hazard with Toby Strange. Having no means of settling this debt, he was forced to sell off some small items of plate that had been brought along with a lot of his other furnishings from London; Giles Brown disposed of the stuff twenty miles away in Garth, and they both devoutly hoped that no one would notice there was anything missing. It was ridiculous that a man should be reduced to the necessity of stealing his own possessions.

"And for all that, I'm not a whit further ahead," John complained. "I've got to meet her privately, away from her father's boon companions. Though the devil knows how I'm to do it, with Sir Bernard watching every move I make."

"There's May Day's Eve," suggested Giles.

John told him crossly not to be a fool, and promptly began to wonder whether May Day's Eve might provide a solution. One factor at least was on his side: he had heard that Toby Strange was going back to London. With his chief rival out of the way, it would be much easier to come to terms with Tamsin.

He made his plans. He discovered that she always went out with the villagers to fetch home the May, and that luckily for him the Sutleigh and Minton people went to the same shoulder of woodland, which lay between their two combes. Having reconnoitred the ground, he sent over one of his grooms with a note requesting her to meet him at a certain time and place. Jenkyn came back to say that the young lady had read the letter, and smiled, and said that if his lordship came into the woods, he would certainly find her there. This was the most propitious sign Tamsin had given him up to now.

And then, about an hour before he was due to start, it was borne in on him that the Ketterings also meant to go Maying, in a family party, and that he was expected to accompany them. Not that they meant to stay out all night; simply to stroll about for a couple of hours, gathering a fair share of the greenery for tomorrow's celebrations. And that couple of hours, John calculated, would bedevil his meeting with Tamsin.

There was nothing to be done. Presently he found himself walking sedately across the water-meadow and into the trees with Bernard, Ann, five of their children (two of whom were going to need carrying before the treat was over) and several of their attendants.

The object was to collect leaves and flowers with which to deck the village maypole and the little bowers that would be set up all round it in the morning. Soon the ladies were hunting for early cowslips, while the men lopped off branches of ash and hazel. The smaller children were plucking up all the weeds that took their fancy and soon wilted in their hot, grasping hands.

"I am a master in this kind of woodcraft," said Bernard. He had stuck a sprig of blackthorn in his cap and was looking very jaunty. "How many years is it since we first went Maying, my love?"

"Twelve," said Ann.

"There you are, John. That's a proof

of devotion: if you can trudge through damp thickets after the same woman for twelve years without complaining."

He picked up Ann's basket and handed it to her with a mock bow which was a very thin disguise of the tenderness he felt towards her.

"You are to be congratulated," said John.

Privately he thought that men of forty ought not to make a parade of being in love with their wives.

There were plenty of other families about, from the farms and cottages, as well as their own servants from the great house; greetings were exchanged, and comparisons with last year — not so many flowers perhaps, but at least the grass was dry. Besides the families, there were the boys and girls skirmishing round each other for partners, sauntering arm in arm, or slipping off between the bushes. Sir Bernard kept a sharp, not to say intimidating eye on them. Once he sailed into the middle of a swarm of youths, extracted two extremely young girls, and packed them off home to their parents.

"That's another reason I came out here," he said, cryptically.

"To play the puritan, sir?"

"To watch over those who are too silly to take care of themselves, and save the parish from undue expense. More bastards get fathered on May Day's Eve than all the other nights in the year put together."

Far away across the combe they heard the teasing call of the cuckoo.

John felt that everything was conspiring to drive him mad: the cuckoo, the amorous village couples, the luminous twilight sky, under which the woodland was becoming as strange and magical as the ocean bed. The puritans who said that May Day was heathen were perfectly right. This night belonged to the old gods, to the pagan tradition which told a man to worship and glorify the sensual world by acting out his delight in the possession of a woman's body.

And he was still half a mile from the place where he had asked Tamsin to meet him half an hour ago.

Ann said: "We ought to turn back. The children are getting tired."

"Let's go as far as the next corner." John had caught an echo of voices which did not seem to belong to rustics.

At the corner two paths crossed, and the two groups suddenly converged. He had been right — this noisy party included half a dozen of the local wild-heads, two giggling daughters of a Sutleigh farmer and Margery and Tamsin — all progressing in a very jolly and informal manner.

They stopped short when they saw the Ketterings. There was a palpable awkwardness. Ann did what she thought of as a Christian duty by saying something civil to Tamsin, and Bernard spoke to one of the men.

Margery, exhilarated by the company she was in, tried to get on more familiar terms with her neighbours.

"I see you are showing Lord Harcourt how we keep our May-games in the West Country. Though there's one custom at least that is common to all places, so we shan't have to teach you that, shall we, my lord?"

John froze. Although he had met Tamsin openly at the wedding, he was

74

not supposed to have met Margery at all. The important thing was to crush the wretched woman's pretensions before she said something which would give him away.

Gazing at the space above her head, he shrugged and replied indifferently, "No doubt Sir Bernard's tenants disport themselves in much the same fashion as mine."

He hardly noticed poor Margery's discomfort, for he had just seen Tamsin's face with the gaiety gone out of it. She looked grave, distressed — was it reproachful? He felt a traitor and a brute.

His cousins were collecting themselves and turning for home. As he moved off with them, Ann said, very audibly, "If Tom Grove must inflict his women on the countryside, he might at least teach them to know their place."

John was torn in two directions; he couldn't abruptly desert his relations, yet it seemed unthinkable to abandon Tamsin and their promised evening together. He got out his knife, and pretended to be cutting another branch. In this way he managed to drop behind the rest. He could hear Tamsin's party following their own path; they were now somewhere downhill on his left. He plunged into the wilderness of briars and bracken, and ran as hard as he could to head them off.

When he saw her, she was standing alone in a drift of bluebells; she had not picked any, but seemed to be just gazing there in a kind of dream.

He shouted her name and ran towards her, realised at the last moment that there was a wide gully of broken ground between them, cleared it by inches, and landed so awkwardly that he had to catch on to her to save himself from falling.

They clung together, laughing, in a sea of bluebells.

"What a clumsy lout I am — I hope I haven't hurt you?"

He was a little breathless, not entirely from running. He had seen the expression that leapt into Tamsin's eyes as he reached her. It was (though even John was not conceited enough to imagine this) the expression of a girl who suddenly found herself caught in the wing-span of a flying demi-god.

She smiled, and asked, "Is that your usual pace, or are you in a hurry?"

"I had to speak with you, to tell you why I couldn't meet you before — well, you can guess how it was, my cousins insisted on making a family ceremony of it, curse them. And then, just now, I wouldn't have spoken so unkindly if Lady Kettering hadn't been there, but she can't abide Margery, and I thought it wiser to discourage her as sharply as I could."

He could not bring himself to admit to Tamsin that he had crept over to Sutleigh without his guardian's knowledge, and that he dared not risk Sir Bernard learning the truth. Better blame the whole episode on Ann's prudery.

Luckily, Tamsin was quite ready to accept his explanation. "I don't wonder your cousin was displeased; Margery should not have spoken to your lordship as she did. It was very impertinent."

He could see Margery, at the edge of the glade, encouraging two of her swains in some kind of horseplay.

"I wish you needn't have come with such a crew. Who is supposed to be your escort?"

"I understand that you were," she retorted. "However, I have provided myself with Hannibal Ruskin — "

"That mooncalf!"

"It is a good, faithful, unassuming mooncalf. I also have my brother Simon, as well as Reuben Corp, our gardener, who is very handy with a cudgel. I trust my retinue meets with your lordship's approval?"

"Yes, it does," said John, choosing to disregard the note of irony as he seized on the meaning of what she had just told him. Having received his letter, she had come to the wood accompanied by three people who had no designs on her themselves, and who could be expected to go quietly away as soon as they were told. He was convinced that tonight she would drop all her evasions, and let him love her as he wanted to.

"My darling, I wish I could stop with you now. I'll have to go and behave like a civil guest, but directly I can escape I'll come back to you, and I'll make you so happy, I swear I will."

He kissed her quickly, and was off through the bracken again, without waiting for her reply.

She watched him go; then stooped and began to pick the flowers that were growing round her feet: fragile bluebells, pale tufts of primroses, and little white windflowers, pointed like stars. She was humming a tune under her breath; gradually some words edged their way in.

My sweet heart, come along, don't you
    hear the fond song,
The sweet notes of the nightingale
    flow?
Don't you hear the fond tale of the
    sweet nightingale
As she sings in the valleys below,
As she sings in the valleys below.

Come, sit yourself down with me on
    the ground,
On this bank where the primroses
    grow.
You shall hear the fond tale of the
    sweet nightingale,
As she sings in the valleys below,
As she sings in the valleys below.

79

Tamsin's voice trailed off into silence. She bunched her flowers together, tying them neatly with scraps of thread.

In the meantime, John had run all the way back to join the Ketterings, who wanted to know what had happened to him.

"I thought I saw a squirrel . . . Why, how is it with you, my poppet? Are you very tired?" He hoisted up his small cousin Jane, and insisted on carrying her the rest of the way home.

He had hoped to retreat unobtrusively as soon as they reached the house, but it was no use; he had to go indoors, and up the great staircase to his bedchamber. Once there, he decided to change his shoes, and also to take a heavy cloak which would be serviceable on the hard ground. Then he dismissed his servants and waited impatiently for the night noises of the household to quieten down.

Presently he decided it was safe to move, and ventured out into the curtained gallery with a taper to guide him. Apparently he had been too hasty, for there was another taper coming towards him.

"John — where are you going?"

"Downstairs to fetch a book," said John promptly.

Bernard held up his light and made an observant survey which included the cloak and shoes.

"You are remarkably well dressed for a journey to the library. Go back into your room."

"Sir — "

"I have a good deal to say to you, and I don't propose to say it out here."

He waited calmly for John to do what he was told, followed him into the bedchamber and shut the door. Having lit the candles from the taper in his hand, he turned and faced his ward.

"You were going to meet a woman. Who was it?"

John did not answer.

"Was it one of our servants?"

"No!" With a burst of indignation.

Bernard thought for a moment. "There was that whore from Sutleigh; I tell you, John, if you've been getting yourself entangled — "

"Oh, for God's sake! Surely you could see what she was after? The pleasure of exchanging a few words with a lord, and boasting of it later to her low friends. But you have to believe the worst of me, don't you? Well, you are wrong, for I haven't had a woman since I came down here, and that's the truth."

The last statement was literally true, thanks to Tamsin's delaying tactics; everything else he had said or implied was so speciously near the wind. He was determined to keep his secret, certain that once Bernard realised where his real interest lay, he would never have a chance of getting near Tamsin again.

In fact, Bernard had already summed up Tamsin as a potential danger at the wedding, but her manner to John had been so off-hand, and John himself had been so cautious in public, that it had looked as though they were immune to each other's attractions.

Bernard pounced on John's last remark. "I take it you are suffering from the wasting sickness?"

"I don't know what you mean."

"The fatal disease of continence. I gather it is now believed to be fatal by any of you young men who are so

82

unfortunate as to live without a mistress for more than a week. So you were sallying forth in search of a remedy, is that it? Any female who would let you lie under a hedge with her. They are five for a farthing in the woods tonight, and an ugly wench is as good as a pretty one in the dark."

Much as he resented this, John had put himself in a position where he had either got to accept it or drag in Tamsin. It was no good pretending that he wasn't going out after a girl of some sort, because Bernard would never believe him, and anyway, he drew the line at deliberate lying. Scowling at the floor, he muttered that it was natural for a man to consort with women.

"And equally natural for him to live in a cave and tear raw meat with his teeth. We are not savages, John; we are redeemed and rational creatures, and we ought not to forget it. There's no sense in putting on that mulish expression because you don't like sermons; this one is directly addressed to your condition. I'm not speaking of your spiritual condition. You are supposed to be capable of examining your own conscience (though I sometimes wonder whether you know the meaning of the word.) I am in charge of your worldly well-being until you come of age, and I notice you do not disdain such unnatural acts as living in a house the size of a palace, or having three hundred servants to wait on you. When it comes to judging a horse or a sonnet, you can refine and discriminate. It is in your sensual pleasures alone that you seem to think you are justified in behaving like an animal. Well, it will not do. At present I can stop you going to Crossingbourne and debauching the daughters of your tenantry — or catching the pox in a Bankside brothel. But one day you will be free from my tutelage, and I warn you. If you don't learn to govern your appetites, they will ruin you. I believe that Tom Grove was as handsome and quick-witted as you are, when he was nineteen."

John shifted his weight from foot to foot, and went as plainly as he dared through the dumbshow of not listening, not believing, not caring. Some token of defiance was essential to shatter the impact of what Bernard had been saying.

Getting one of his lectures was always a lacerating experience. This one appeared to be over. He said: "I'll leave you to your reflections — and I hope to a sound rest. You can give me your word that you will not go out again tonight."

"My word? Surely that's not necessary." John had every intention of going out, and he was not going to tie himself down by making promises.

"It is not precisely necessary. If you refuse, I shall lock you in."

"You will do *what?*"

Bernard did not answer. Suiting the action to the threat, he crossed the room in a leisurely fashion and took the big iron key out of the door. He paused, glancing at his ward.

"You heard what I said. Which is it to be?"

John was bristling with all the protests that he wanted to make about the unjust and unseemly way he was being treated, but his native caution kept him quiet. Once he got into an argument, he might find himself saddled with some half-promise he didn't wish to keep. If he could stick to his refusal, Bernard would lock him in, and then he could climb out of the window. All the same, it was a harsh blow to his pride.

Bernard said, "You are an obstinate whelp, aren't you, John? I suppose I shall teach you manners in time. Heaven knows who will teach you sense."

He went out, turning the lock behind him with a series of twists and clicks which sounded deliberately malicious to his cousin, a prisoner inside his own bedchamber.

A furious and baffled prisoner who could not now imagine what had induced him to stand by so meekly, when he might have got the key away from Bernard by force. Except, of course, that he would have been beaten before he started.

He was afraid of Bernard.

Not physically afraid, or hardly at all; it was a sense of personal inferiority which he was unable to exorcise. The complicated pattern of dependence and obedience had existed since he was a child.

Born to a wonderful inheritance, he had not been especially lucky in his family. His father had died when he was six; his mother and her second husband were weak and foolish. He soon learnt to wind them round his finger with contemptuous ease. And the succession of tutors, chaplains and so forth was worthy but not inspiring. The one man who roused him to wild enthusiasm and hero-worship was his splendid soldier cousin. It was unlucky that the only person he really valued was also the only one who ever punished him at all severely or told him any painful home truths. Perhaps it was natural that by now his function in John's life seemed to be rather like the Voice of God in the mystery plays.

"But he has no right to treat me as though I was twelve years old," said John aloud. He went across to the window, pulled back the curtains, opened the casement, and levered himself on to the narrow sill. It was a risky attempt but he was so desperate to get out that he didn't care. His room was on the first floor, and he reckoned he could dangle his way down the ornamental façade of the house and jump.

He then discovered that he could not get through the window. He was a very slim young man, but too long in the limb to fold himself up small, and his broad shoulders would never go through that cramped space. He swore and squeezed and sweated for a bit, but in the end he had to give it up.

He was frantic with mortification and temper. He could actually see the bonfires and torches of the revellers out there in the dark, and hear faint sounds which he thought he could identify as music and laughter. Somewhere out there Tamsin was waiting for him, puzzled and disappointed because he did not come. Or perhaps she had given up waiting and consoled herself.

It was intolerable. He flung himself face downwards on the bed, thumping the pillows with his clenched fists, and pouring out a stream of the most vicious invective he knew in a low, repetitive monotone. It was an impenitently natural man whom Bernard had shut up like an animal in a cage.

May

THERE was a long-standing tradition that the people of Minton and Sutleigh joined together to furnish the same may-pole and danced round it together on the short grass in front of the church at Minton Gabriel — a custom that was said to go back two hundred and fifty years to the time after the Black Death when there were not enough men left in either village to put up a maypole on their own.

No one had thought of mentioning this to John, so that his first thought, when he woke up on May Day morning, was that he would not see Tamsin, because they would both be dutifully bound to take part in their own local celebrations. He was rather relieved. He had no idea what excuse he could make to explain why he had not gone back to her in the wood, and he certainly wasn't going to tell her the ignominious truth.

He got out of bed and discovered that his door was now unlocked. Bernard must have done that in the small hours; at least he was not going to be disgraced in front of his own servants.

He was feeling very disconsolate and ill-used when he went downstairs to join the rest of the household, though they were all much too self-absorbed to notice — which did not improve his temper. The chaplain said prayers as usual, and then they all trooped out into the sunshine.

On the rough track below the forecourt, waiting for the Kettering family to arrive, were a large party of villagers, formed up in marching order and wearing their best clothes. The centre-piece of this procession was a couple of wagons roped together, and lengthwise along the top of them, jutting out at each end, the trunk of a great tree. The branches had been lopped off, leaving raw, white wounds but these were hardly visible for the whole surface of the tree had been entwined and festooned with leaves. The long swathes of greenery were poked through at every intersection, and yards of coloured ribbon were looped through the knots. Harnessed to the wagons were eight teams of oxen, all groomed and sleek, with garlands over their broad shoulders, and nosegays of cowslips and primroses at the tips of their horns.

"That's a sight I love to see," said Bernard. "The devil run away with Philip Stubbes and his notion of stinking idols." He spoke in a friendly, casual way to John, as if to show that last night's episode could be forgotten. "Come — we shall be required to make a tour of inspection."

As they moved forward, John suddenly saw Tamsin. She was quite close, standing on the hub of one of the wheels, and reaching across to tuck in some foliage that had come adrift. In that setting, and dressed in vivid green, with her red lips and her creamy skin, she looked a glorious and unashamed pagan. Her eyes caught John's for a second, then she finished what she was doing and jumped down from the wheel, ignoring the various arms that reached out to help her.

John had stopped. Someone trod on

his heels and apologised. He moved on, inevitably, towards Tamsin, and heard Bernard congratulating her on decorations; she seemed to be in some way responsible.

"I thank you, Sir Bernard. Do you like oxen? They remind me of bridesmaids."

Bernard burst out laughing. "I suppose there are points of comparison — but do remember it was you who found them, Mrs. Grove. I should never have dared to be so unchivalrous."

Not too virtuous to banter wits with a pretty wanton when his wife did not happen to be listening, thought John sourly. Bernard started talking to the ploughboys who were in charge of the oxen, and Tamsin turned her attention to John.

"What became of you last night, my lord?"

This was what he dreaded, and he had no answer prepared; had not realised until a few seconds ago that there was any risk of seeing her today.

Pretending to examine the flowers on the maypole, he muttered out of the corner of his mouth, "I changed my plans. That is — it was not convenient."

"I suppose you didn't happen to consider my convenience?"

"I'm very sorry, Tamsin. But it's a matter we can't discuss here."

"Why not?" Everyone was chattering all round them, they could talk quite safely under the protection of the noise. She tried to imagine what it was that could not be discussed. "Did you have the colic?"

"No, I did not!" snapped John, revolted at this insult.

He was unhappy and on the defensive, and he decided, rather unwisely, to take refuge in the careless grandeur of a young nobleman who could do exactly what he pleased.

"If you want the truth," he drawled, without the slightest intention of telling it, "we drank a cup of wine or so, and the time passed quicker than I thought. Until it hardly seemed worth returning to that infernally dark wood. After all, there are plenty of other places. And we shall deal better together, my love, if we aren't freezing cold."

If she didn't like that answer, she

shouldn't ask so many questions. John had never exactly formulated the belief that whoever he made love with, he was the one who was conferring the benefit. But the idea was somewhere in the back of his mind, and he thought that Tamsin would do well to stop pestering him; she would have nothing to complain of in the long run.

In fact, she did not make any comment at all, for by now the oxen were heaving forward, braced against the weight of their load, the men were shouting encouragement, and she was busy marshalling the village children into their places beside the first wagon. After a moment's hesitation, John went to join his cousin at the head of the procession.

Tamsin's feelings as she watched him had nothing to do with the warm, sweet-scented burgeonings of springtime, or the prodigal generosity of young love. She had never been so angry in her life.

Of course she did not believe that story about the cup or so of wine, and the time passing quickly. No one in their senses would credit that as a literal account of how he had ended the evening which, a few hours earlier, he had wanted to spend in her arms. He had presumably got so drunk that he was incapable of coming back to find her. Or else — and this was more likely, from what she knew of him — he had got drunk enough to decide that it was easier to single out one of the Minton servingmaids, who was there on the spot in a warm, dry house, instead of trudging across country for Tamsin Grove. After all, an obliging girl like Tamsin could be taken for granted any night of the week. 'Deal better together if we aren't freezing cold' indeed! I'll deal with you, my lord, she promised bitterly.

She had not many illusions. No one who had grown up at Sutleigh could have failed to learn that men frequently got drunk and ran after any female in sight. But she had never before met anyone so glaringly inconstant, anyone who could pursue her so greedily, let himself be deflected so easily, and then come back to her with scarcely a word of regret, assuming that he could take possession when and where he pleased. It made no difference to him that she might have hung around all night, entirely to do his bidding. He certainly had not realised that she never went to bed on May Day's Eve because she and several of the farmers' wives were in charge of all the stuff that had to be sorted out, woven into garlands and so on. Spoilt young demi-gods like Lord Harcourt probably thought that maypoles dressed themselves at four in the morning without human aid. Well, how could she expect him to care whether she helped to deck the maypole or not? As far as he was concerned, she had one sole function, and apart from that she would hardly exist for him as a living human creature.

They had reached the deep hole which had been dug for the maypole on a flat sweep of land between the church and the river. An expert band of woodcutters manoeuvred the pole into position, levered it upright with ropes, and got it firmly planted. As the crowd fanned out on to the surrounding grass, Tamsin caught a clear glimpse of John Harcourt, so outstandingly tall and graceful. In a queer way it hurt her to look at this beautiful and quite insufferable young man. He had a very sullen expression today. Until now she had let herself be dazzled by his charm, but behind it there was a spoilt egotist whom she disliked more than anyone she had ever met.

The villagers had formed a huge circle and were dancing a hey-de-gay round the maypole. Eight paces to the left they went, then eight to the right. Arms entwined, the couples bobbing round each other like apples in a bucket of water. All the intricate patterns and interlocking chains, to the music of the pipe and tabor.

The gentry were not supposed to dance with the common people. They sat sedately in bowers made of hurdles and thatched with green branches that were already beginning to droop in the hot sun. Tamsin sat with the Mulcasters; neither her father nor Margery had come to the May-games. John gazed anxiously across at her. In retrospect his excuses seemed unsatisfying, and he was afraid she must think he had behaved very inconsistently. Presently the wrestling and archery began at the far side of the meadow. The dancers thinned out a little as some of them went to watch. Quite soon Tamsin and several of the Mulcasters got up and left their bower; John waited a short while and then followed them.

Tamsin had a special interest in the archery contest, because her half-brother Simon was shooting for Sutleigh. Although he was only fourteen, Simon was big and heavy for his age, and he could already handle the English longbow like a grown man.

This was a prick-shooting match, a test of accuracy rather than strength, for they were using light arrows over a fairly short distance. There were five archers a side; when John joined the spectators, one of the Minton men had just finished his first flight with two hits out of three, and it was Simon's turn to shoot. He wandered over in that rather slouching way that made his elders say he was inattentive and disrespectful; he was adjusting his arm-guard, and pulling the leather shooting-glove over the first three fingers of his right hand. He saw no reason to worry; eight score was a trivial distance by his standards. However, when he had fitted his shaft, he took a careful aim at the mark, a canvas pad stuffed with straw; there was a painted white disc in the middle, and a peg stuck in the centre of the disc. Simon drew back his arm. The shaft streaked invisibly through the air and hit the white. The second time he hit the white again. The final shaft of the flight quivered as it landed, and there was a sharp little crack at the impact. He had split the pin.

There was a burst of approval; even the Minton people could not refrain from giving their rival a small cheer. John had not met Simon on his one visit to the Manor. He turned to Kettering's gentleman-usher, a rather obtuse man called Henry Lembridge, who was standing next to him.

"Who is that?"

"One of Tom Grove's bastards, my lord."

Tamsin heard the loud and cheerful reply; she was always a vulnerable target for such arrows of thoughtless cruelty. She dismissed the speaker from her mind; Henry Lembridge was a person of no consequence whatever. But it was intolerable of John Harcourt to have asked the question that led to such an answer; she disliked him more than ever.

John was making his way towards her now.

"Your brother is a splendid bowman. I wish I could shoot as well as he does."

"I did not know that gentlemen of your lordship's eminence condescended to use such a weapon."

John was mildly surprised. He wondered whether to remind her that Henry VIII had been the best archer in the kingdom, but decided against it. He could guess what was annoying her, poor sweet, and it had nothing to do with archery.

"When can I see you again?" he asked urgently.

Tamsin did not answer.

"Will you let me take you to Garth next week, to see the players?"

"I think it is too far."

"A mere twenty miles? These fellows ply their trade very well for a travelling company; one particular rogue is an old acquaintance of mine ... Do say you will come."

When she still refused, he said, "Well, we don't need a set of mummers to divert us, after all. I had rather be alone with you in any meeting-place of your own choosing."

Tamsin hesitated. A most entertaining and splendid plan had just flashed into her brain. It was too much to hope for, she would never bring it off — still, it was worth trying.

"Do you know Wilfred's Tower?"

"That old ruin on the hill at the top of your combe? I've seen it often from a distance."

"If you were to ride up tomorrow, about three in the afternoon, I could be there," she said, in the off-hand manner of someone conceding a victory without admitting it.

She ventured a quick glance at him to see how he was taking this. The mixture of apparent cajoling and uncertainty affected him strangely; he found his heart thumping.

"I'll be there," he said.

It was always the same; girls were

like spaniels. Neglect them, trample on their feelings, and they ran after you and begged for attention. Last night's misfortune was turning out for the best after all.

★ ★ ★

Wilfred's Tower was a mysterious old ruin that stood high on the hill at the apex of Sutleigh Combe. John had always been vaguely conscious of it, sticking up on the skyline like a broken tooth. There was a big stack of brushwood up there, kept permanently ready for lighting, in case the Spaniards came again, as they had in eighty-eight. Apparently the shepherds used the place too, as a sheepfold in bad weather, for as John came close he saw there was a pen of hurdles against one wall of the tower. And tied to a hurdle was a small grey gelding, peacefully grazing.

So she had arrived.

It was a brilliant blue and green afternoon, hot for the time of year, though there was a little tugging breeze at this height, like the wind in the tall sails of a ship at sea. Just round the tower there was a turf clearing; beyond that, the inevitable tangle of bramble and bracken. As John drew rein, Tamsin's head and shoulders appeared behind a gorse bush, and she stood up. She had evidently been sitting on the ground, watching his approach. He dismounted, tethered his horse, and went to meet her.

"Well, my sweet? I've followed you to the ends of the earth, very nearly. Are you pleased to see me?"

"Honoured, my lord." She parried his outstretched hands with her own, using them as a last little barrier of restraint. When he began to kiss her, she laughed gently, and said, "Not yet, Harcourt. I am not ready."

"What a procrastinating girl you are. When will you be ready?"

"All in due course. Do you know the history of this place?"

"Wilfred's Tower?" He looked the building over indifferently. It was certainly ancient and had been partly destroyed, probably by men who wanted to use the stone, for the remaining walls were stout enough, uncorrupted by the elements.

"Has it a history? Who was Wilfred?"

"Some Saxon king or other. But he doesn't matter. It's the hill, don't you feel how wild it is up here? It used to be — unlawful to build shrines in high places."

Witchcraft? Was that what she was hinting at? He studied the tower with rather more interest, but was unable to feel any particular sense of evil.

"They say," continued Tamsin, "that the man who climbs Wilfred's Tower can climb into any bed in the kingdom."

"Was that why you brought me here?" asked John, amused. He had never found much difficulty about the beds he wanted to climb into.

"We in Sutleigh like to prove what our lovers are worth."

He stared at her in astonishment. She appeared to be quite serious. Could she be so simple-minded that she insisted on going through all the courtship rituals of her native village, like an illiterate peasant? It seemed hardly possible. Unless she got an added excitement from invoking the powers that were supposed to haunt this place? There had been a touch of provocation in her use of the word unlawful . . . There were women, the very reverse of simple-minded, who would do odd things to heighten the taste of pleasure. He had not imagined that Tamsin was one of them, and felt an illogical pang of disappointment. After all, it was what he wanted: a mistress who knew every move of the game.

"What am I supposed to do?"

"Simply to climb the Tower. But perhaps your lordship has no head for heights — " She left the sentence delicately unfinished.

"Have your other lovers done this?" he asked abruptly. "Toby Strange, for instance?"

"Oh, Toby!" The soft laugh seemed reminiscent, the black eyes a little derisive. "He's not one to hang back asking questions. Toby is a man — " slight pause for emphasis in order to draw comparisons " — who doesn't mind risking his neck to get what he desires."

That settled it. He would climb the damned Tower, and then he would come down and take this little Jezebel into the bracken and show her whether he was man enough to master her.

He removed his hat, jacket and ruff, laying them on the ground, and kicked off his riding-boots. Without taking any further notice of Tamsin, he started his assault on the Tower. It was not at all difficult, for there were plenty of finger-holds and ledges in the rough chunks of stone. Right foot up to the level of the left knee; bring the left foot up to join it, let the toes grope for support. Now hoist upwards to find a new handgrip. The sharp air in his lungs and the gritty surface of the wall reminded him of climbs in his boyhood. For him, there was nothing satanic or erotic about this performance. If Tamsin enjoyed watching him, he had no objection. He was a remarkably fine athlete and he knew it.

He got triumphantly to the top, and rested, gazing at the view. The great, smooth hills, and the secret, woody combes, stretching away westwards to a horizon that might be either mist or sea. Much closer were the tiny houses of Sutleigh. Closer still, Tamsin was standing just below the Tower, smiling and waving. He waved back, and began the descent, agreeably stimulated.

He was about two-thirds of the way down when he heard some jinglings and rustlings from the sheepfold where the horses were tethered. He could not look just then, but he had an idea that one of them must have got loose, and that Tamsin was trying to catch it. As soon as he had got himself wedged into a safe crevice, he turned his head sideways and looked down.

What he saw nearly made him fall off the Tower.

Both the horses were now untied. Tamsin was back in the saddle of her own grey, and holding the reins of his Barbary mare in her spare hand. As John gaped at her, stupefied, she trotted briskly off down the hill, riding one horse and leading the other.

"No!" he shouted. "Hi! Tamsin — what are you doing?"

He did not wait to see whether she would answer or look back. He almost slid down the side of the Tower in his haste, landed on his hands and knees, picked himself up and ran idiotically down the hill, shouting, though the girl and the horses had now vanished between the trees.

It was hopeless. Once he realised that, he came to a halt, breathless, bewildered, and so angry that for some time he could do nothing but just stand there raging.

"Bitch!" he said aloud. "Lying, cheating, false-hearted bitch!"

What right or reason had she got to play such a trick on him? He could scarcely believe that any girl would dare to treat him so badly. Least of all this ignorant, mannerless, base-born provincial slut who ought to be grateful to him for wanting to waste a single hour on her. Which he wouldn't have done if the choice hadn't been so limited.

It was no good staying here and sulking. He had got to get himself home, and the first move was to find his clothes and put them on. He returned to the Tower and spent some time hunting around before the horrid truth dawned on him. Tamsin had not merely stolen his horse, she had also purloined his hat, doublet, ruff and boots.

This time he was speechless, there were

no names bad enough.

He was wearing a shirt of fine white lawn, dark green breeches, and a pair of woven yellow stockings; no one could say that he was not decently dressed — but on the other hand, no one could possibly expect to see him anywhere outside his bedchamber in such a costume. He had already realised that he would have to walk the whole five miles to Minton and then account for himself by inventing a convenient riding accident. But how to account for his missing clothes. What could he say he had been doing? He knew at once what Bernard would think he had been doing, and was filled with gloom.

As he tramped down the hill, he seemed to be the only man alive. He found it very painful walking without shoes, for the little sheep-tracks he had to follow were thorny underfoot and littered with trailing briars, and when he wasn't pulling vicious needles out of the soles of his stockings, he was stubbing his toes or twisting his ankles in the hidden ruts. It was a penance to walk in such conditions, and slowed him down considerably.

He had soon left the high breeze behind, and the combe was like a bakehouse. Now he had to trudge upwards again, to get over the saddle of land that divided Sutleigh from Minton. He managed to lose his way and wasted a good deal of energy walking round in circles. The sun glared through the trees; the wood was hot, dense and oppressive.

At last he emerged thankfully into the meadow where the rather bedraggled maypole was still standing. There were some cottages on the left, he hoped there was no one looking out. He was so carefully keeping his eye on the cottages, that he forgot to safeguard his other side, and was petrified by a shrill scream about two yards away on his right. He swung round and encountered a little girl of about eight, who was goggling at him with a mixture of surprise and terror. For a few seconds they were both paralysed; then the child ran off towards the cottages, still screaming, and John retreated hurriedly into the wood.

He came to a huge old holly bush; kneeling on the ground, he wriggled his way under the lower branches to the heart of it. He got nearly scratched to death in the process, but he had to put up with that and make use of the best refuge he could get, for he was sure that they would come to search for him.

And he was right. A few minutes later he heard voices on the edge of the wood.

"'Twere a naked man, I tell 'ee. Our Doll she did see 'un plain as plain. Half-naked, leastways, with bare arms and bare feet. I reckon he can't 'a' gone far."

"One of they Tom o' Bedlams, like as not, that do rant around the country, preying on decent folk."

"I'll not have any heathen loonytick scaring my little maid."

John listened, holding his breath, while the men ranged all round him, shaking the bushes and prodding the undergrowth, at the same time discussing what they would do with the contemptible creature who went about frightening poor little maids. They would thrash him soundly, throw him in the horse-pond, hand him over to the constable or, better still, take him to the great house for Sir Bernard to deal with.

He had a bad moment when someone suggested fetching a dog, but nothing came of it; the men were all anxious to get back to their work in the fields, and after a while they went away and left him alone under his holly bush. He crept out, but was too nervous to venture into the meadow again; the people at the cottages had been thoroughly roused, he could hear the women all out gossiping on their doorsteps. And even if he braved those cottages, there was the rest of the village, and after that the great house itself, surrounded by wide, flat gardens, with sixty-five windows surveying every inch of the terrain. He was dirty, thirsty, footsore; the heat of his long walk had drained out of him, and the sweat was drying cold and clammy under his once immaculate shirt. He could see no prospect of getting back into the house until it was dark. He sat on a tree-stump and thought of what he would like to do to Tamsin Grove.

He had been sitting there for over an hour when he heard the sound of hoofbeats coming along the nearest ride.

He got up and moved silently forward, to peer through the branches at the passing horseman — and for once his luck was in.

"Giles!"

Giles Brown stopped and looked round. "My dear lord, what's happened? Are you hurt?" He was full of horrified concern.

"There's nothing the matter with me, but I need some clothes. You must go to the house and fetch me a hat and doublet and some boots, and bring them to me here. Oh, and a ruff — "

"Thank God you're safe. When they told me the Barbary mare had trotted into the yard without you, I was afraid you might have broken your neck."

"The mare's back, is she? Does my cousin know?"

"Not yet. He's out visiting some of his tenants. But the steward was beginning to talk of a search-party, and knowing where you'd gone, I thought you'd prefer me to make a search on my own. I thought that if Tamsin was with you — what's become of Tamsin?" He eyed his master with undisguised curiosity. "How did you lose your coat and boots?"

"That same way I lost my horse." It was no good making up stories, he never kept anything from Giles. "That strumpet went off with them all, and left me adrift on the hillside."

"She must be raving mad! Why should she do such a thing?"

"Good God, Giles, do you think I can read her mind? I suppose she finds some strange diversion in leading men on and making fools of them."

"Oh!" said Giles, who had suddenly grasped the point. "Do you mean to say she never let you — well, I do call that shabby, my lord."

"I don't care what you call it. And take that smirk off your face, confound you. I won't have you laughing."

"I do assure your lordship — it's no laughing matter," said Giles in a strangled voice. His manner was portentously grave, but it was obvious that he could hardly keep a straight face.

John was obliged to control his fury. He was depending on Giles to get him some clothes.

★ ★ ★

Giles went stealthily back to the house and fetched the necessary garments, without which John was beginning to feel literally naked.

Properly dressed, he was able to stroll through the village, and arrive at the forecourt of the great house just as Bernard and some of the men were setting out to look for him. It was easy to talk about a fall; Bernard took this as one of the natural risks that everybody had to run, and was simply glad he hadn't broken any bones.

John went upstairs to wash and change for supper. He kept Giles to wait on him and sent his other servants away, so that he could speak his mind, which he did with such extreme freedom that Giles began to feel decidedly worried. He could only hope that a companionable evening in the Kettering family circle would have a calming effect.

By a perversity of fate, Sir Bernard had letters to write, so John was able to retire to his bedchamber much earlier than usual; he ordered Giles to get a

115

bottle of wine, and sat there drinking it and plotting mischief.

"It's going on for dusk; another five minutes and I'll be off. You did tell them to saddle Nero?"

"Yes, my lord, but I do wish you wouldn't go — "

"And you must remember," said John, interrupting him, "to slip down after everyone is in bed, and open that window in the parlour so that I can get in again."

"I wish you'd let this enterprise alone, for tonight at any rate."

"Why?"

Giles looked at him, flushed and restless, with a hectic light of excitement in his eyes. "For one reason, you're three parts drunk."

"What of it? You can't say I shall be out of place at Sutleigh."

"Maybe not, but you are so wildly impulsive. John, do consider for a moment!" Giles reverted to the Christian name terms of their shared childhood, a liberty he very rarely allowed himself now. "What will you gain by visiting the girl in her father's house? She'll call on her friends to throw you out, and you'll end by kicking up a most unsavoury scandal. Sir Bernard will be certain to hear of it."

"I don't care," said John, full of Dutch courage. "I'm going to Sutleigh tonight, and you needn't ask what I hope to achieve, for you know very well, only you're too squeamish to say so."

This was partly the obstinacy of a spoilt child who could not bear to be thwarted, and partly the bravado that came out of a bottle. When he drank too much, which wasn't often, the fumes always flew straight to his brain and his temper, inflaming his judgment, but leaving him physically unaffected, except for a pleasant sense of well-being. In this state he could never put a foot wrong. His departure from Minton and the ride across the hill passed swiftly and successfully like a dream, a complete contrast to the tedious miseries of the afternoon. He was still tingling with anger and a longing for revenge, but he had worked himself to the stage where these feelings were a positive enjoyment.

Arrived at Sutleigh, he was sober

enough to take his horse round by the outbuildings and leave him in an empty barn. He approached the house across a stretch of rough grass, treading so softly that none of the dogs barked. (Though he might have counted on that; in this down-at-heel and irregular household, even the watchdogs were badly trained).

There was a lighted window. Standing well back in the shadows, he looked in. A boy was sitting at a table, writing, or rather holding a quill in his hand, and poring over his foolscap with an expression of dogged apathy. John recognised Tamsin's brother Simon, the young archer. He moved to the next window; here was a more interesting scene. Tom Grove, lolling in his chair, already fuddled for the evening. His red-headed mistress entertaining Matt Webber, who was obviously about to console her; they were very close to each other on the settle. Gregory Timberlake, a little apart, was casting dice, right hand against left. There was no sign of Tamsin.

He walked round to the front of the house, tried the door, which was unbolted, and went in. No one challenged him. He went up the shallow oak staircase. There was a room at the top which was obviously the master's chamber. In most families, the daughters slept in the room beyond their parents. But not, thought John, this daughter and this parent. He rambled his way carefully through various empty apartments all leading out of each other; the curtains were not drawn, so it was just possible to see. At last he found what he had been looking for; a closed door with a glimmer of light shining underneath it. He was pleased to note that it was as far as possible from the people downstairs.

He opened the door without knocking and went in.

Tamsin was sitting on the edge of her bed, reading a book by the light of a candle. Her hair drifted down her shoulders with the blackness of velvet. She was in her smock, with a cream silk gown over it, exaggerating the long slender lines of her body.

For an instant she watched him coming towards her, her dark eyes widening, her lips parted in a small O of astonishment.

Then she said clearly, "Get out of here."

John laughed. No words would have made his answer more threatening.

She jumped up, and the book fell on the floor. "If you touch me, I'll scream."

"Scream, then. No one will hear you."

He took her by the shoulders, and she did let out a cry of anger and protest which would have alarmed him if he had been sober, but in fact he was right: nobody could hear her.

He gave her a sharp slap which shocked her into silence, and tightened his bruising grip on the soft flesh of her upper arms. She was delightfully fragile and vulnerable without the stiff boning of a stomacher and farthingale, and she couldn't do much kicking this time, she had bare feet. He forced her to stand still while he kissed her as long and as hard as he wanted to.

When at last she managed to drag her mouth away from his, she was ready to beg for terms. "Harcourt, for God's sake — let me go!"

"You can go when you've had your lesson, and not before. You're going to be taught what happens to impudent little whores who break their promises."

"But I made you no promise," she cried desperately.

He pushed her across the bed and held her down while she struggled.

Tamsin felt as though she was drowning in a sea of humiliation and fear and violent physical sensation. It was altogether monstrous that she was going to be raped by this boy because she had goaded him too far, because he didn't understand . . .

She was still trying to appeal to him as he knelt over her and began to take off her smock, but she knew that at this point he was beyond listening. She had managed to get one hand free, and she seized the only weapon within reach, which happened to be the candlestick, and tried to hit him with it. The feeble blow glanced off his back, the candle fell on to the pillow, and a sudden jet of flame shot up one of the bed-curtains in a petrifying yellow flare.

John raised his head, blinked, and came out of his devil's nightmare. This broke the spell as nothing else could — a still more primal instinct took charge. He jumped off the bed, picked Tamsin up and dumped her behind him on the ground. Then he caught hold of the burning curtain and tore it away from the framework of the bed; it was a difficult and painful job, with the flames licking out at him, but he knew what had to be done. He managed to keep his head averted, dragged the curtain down on to the floor, rolled it into a heap and trod on it.

The pillow was still smouldering; he threw that after the curtain and stamped on it as well. A few little fragments of material floated upwards in luminous curls of fire that withered and vanished.

Tamsin arrived at his side with a pitcher of water. He took it from her and poured some over the charred debris, which finally doused any lurking flames. There was a hissing noise and a horribly sour, pungent smell that caught them both high in the throat and made them choke.

John put down the jug and straightened up; he was not much the worse, though he had scorched his doublet and burnt his hands quite badly pulling on the curtain. Now that he had made them wet, the stinging of his palms was the most excruciating agony, and for a few seconds he could think of nothing else. But the actual intensity of the pain pierced the mists of wine and temper and wounded pride in which he had been luxuriating, and all at once he was quite clear-headed and deadly cold. He looked around, like an awakened sleepwalker. There was still one candle alight, enough to show the feminine details of the room he had invaded, the combs and trinkets on the dressing-chest; the tumbled bed, and the sodden stuff on the floor. He was appalled. Whatever the girl might be, whatever she had done, nothing excused the way he had behaved in the past few minutes.

There were some furtive movements behind him. Tamsin had taken a long cloak from behind the door, and was huddling herself inside its effacing folds. He turned, and saw her watching him out of the eyes of a frightened child. The reproach in those eyes was unbearable — and it had no connection with his

123

image of the young woman he had been hating all the afternoon.

He said, "I'm sorry. I should not have — have used you as I did. I let my anger carry me too far."

She did not speak.

"Is there anything you need, that I can do for you?"

"Only to leave me alone, my lord." It was a bloodless whisper, without tone or feeling.

"You've nothing more to fear. I'll leave you in peace. I don't make a habit of ravishing girls who don't want me. I've never before in my life attempted to take a woman against her will."

He could not tell, from what he could see of her face in the shadows, whether Tamsin believed this. Her hands plucked at the borders of her cloak. He was miserably conscious of her distress, knew that she was longing to be rid of him, but at the same time he was so bewildered by his own actions that he had to try and explain.

"It was because you were so unkind to me — I still don't know what I've done to displease you."

"Don't you, my lord?" she enquired, with a slight return of animation.

He flinched. "I wasn't speaking of tonight; I know I have sunk myself for ever. But you must have disliked me already the way you mocked and made a fool of me. For some reason I wasn't fit to be your lover, though you never told me why."

"There's a simple answer. I don't take lovers."

He stared at her, uncomprehending. He couldn't think what she meant. That she wasn't promiscuous, that she was faithful to one man at a time?

"Toby Strange," he began, but she interrupted him.

"No," she said categorically. "Whatever you may have been told."

John was at a loss. He supposed she must be trying to reform, anxious to escape from those tendencies which he had taken for granted ever since their first meeting. Another possibility occurred to him, almost too dreadful to contemplate.

One question had become unavoidable. He had to ask it much as he shrank from the answer. His mouth was dry, and he could hardly recognise his own voice.

"Tamsin, you must tell me — are you a virgin?"

She drew a sharp breath. "What sort of a fabulous beast is that? Have you ever seen one?"

John had not been very intelligent in his dealings with Tamsin, but he had at last learnt to interpret the means she used to protect herself against a dangerous world.

"Oh, my God!" he said, and sat down on the bed. He felt sick at the thought of what he had been trying to do.

For a few moments neither of them moved. He was by now so overcome with shame that he could not bring himself to look at her or speak. He knew there were things he had got to say, but what possible form of words would be adequate?

He was so obviously at a loss that Tamsin began to gain a little courage, and looking at him more observantly she noticed for the first time how he had burnt himself.

"Your hands!" she exclaimed. "You

must be suffering torments. I'll have to dress them for you."

"It's of no account," he muttered, rather surprised by the hot and puckered red bars that were now ridged on the palms of his hands, for he had almost forgotten the pain. He was indeed suffering torments, but of a different kind.

Tamsin unlocked a small chest where she kept various household remedies, and took out a jar of ointment. The prospect of something that needed doing had a tonic effect on her; she had stopped trembling and felt strangely calm, if a little unreal. There was an awkwardness about having to touch him, after their recent contact, but she got over it when she saw that he was far more nervous and reluctant than she was.

She told him briskly to open his hands, and dabbed on the thick, sweet-smelling unguent with impersonal fingers. John was as passive as a child. He would have to sit and let the ointment dry; if he kept it on all night, he would have nothing worse than a few blisters in the morning.

"There. How does that feel?"

"Like coals of fire," said John in a low voice.

Staring at the floor, he had just seen the book which had fallen there during their struggle. He now knew that when he broke into her room, Tamsin had been reading the Bible. This was the final straw.

"I — I don't know what I'm to say to you. What's the use of telling you I'm sorry; what sort of compensation is that? Yet I am deeply sorry, I'd give anything to recall the last hour ... If only I'd known! All these times we've met, why did you never tell me?"

"Is it necessary for an unmarried woman to furnish proofs of her chastity before your lordship will grant her a safe conduct?"

She could not resist the small cruelty. He had been very white before; now he flushed scarlet, as though she had struck him across the face.

"You needn't answer that," she said. "I know it isn't every woman you see in that light. But I'm a bastard — that's different, isn't it? You say to yourself, 'she's bound to be a whore, like her mother.'"

"That's not so!" he protested, rather uncertainly.

"   Then what other reason did you have to take me for a wanton? Oh, I know there are stories — but do you believe them, rather than the evidence of your own eyes? Have you seen me do anything wrong, with any man whatever?"

John was in a quandary. He had behaved atrociously to this girl; how could he add insult to injury by telling her what he thought of her public manners and her associates?

In the end, he said, "I think your friends are somewhat ill-chosen, and that you should not condone all they do with such open complacency. It is natural for strangers to assume that birds of a feather flock together."

"They are my father's friends."

"Then you ought not to be living in your father's house."

"And where else should I go?"

He was taken aback. He had vaguely thinking that plenty of girls had disreputable fathers without themselves being in any way contaminated or touched by scandal: it only now struck him that Tamsin's position might be more complicated.

"Yes," she said, reading his thoughts. "That is the true penalty of my state. Do you suppose I should have been left with him if my parents had been married? Can't you guess what would have happened after my mother's death, when he started to install his Bankside fancies and his boon companions? A tribe of grandparents and uncles and aunts would have descended on us, and whisked me away to be brought up in one of their own families. They would have arranged a suitable match for me, and I should not have seen my father again until I was safely married, and then only if my husband gave me permission. A girl who is guarded so carefully does not stand in much peril. But I don't have grandparents, Lord Harcourt, nor uncles and aunts either. Bastards have no kin. And the Groves certainly don't want me; they will never acknowledge that Simon and I have the smallest claim on the Sutleigh estate, while as for the

Trelawneys, my mother's people, they resent the fact that I was born at all, because of the disgrace I brought on her. So I am more or less compelled to stay where I am and make the best of it."

"Yes. I see. I had not properly considered — it was stupid of me."

"You accuse me of being too tolerant of the company I keep — "

"That was an impertinence. Forget I said so; I did not mean it."

"I think you did, my lord. And I've no doubt you are right." Staring through him at the opposite wall, Tamsin talked quickly in a brittle, scornful voice that just choked back the tears. "I've no doubt I am sometimes too — too free in my conduct, and if I have misled you I beg your pardon. I suppose I ought to stay up here and keep myself unsullied from the gamblers and drunkards and adulterers downstairs. Well, I can't do it. I have managed to live virtuously, but I cannot live like a hermit. These people are all I have. I am attached to my father, and whatever his faults he is kind to me; would it be dutiful to look down my nose at him or preach sermons? Would it be generous to keep on pointing out to Margery that I am an honest woman while she is a strumpet? Poor Margery, what chance has she ever had of being anything else? She was born in a brothel. If she has convinced herself that I give my favours as easily as she does, can you wonder at it? And if Toby and a few of the others go on hoping, what's the harm in that? I am safe enough; they would none of them make love to me without my consent. They are commonplace fellows after all, not members of the nobility."

This thrust hurt as much as she meant it to. And she had completely disarmed him; all his glib reproaches had been silenced by the honest strength of her charity.

"You are so good," he murmured, reversing his previous judgment, and overlooking, in his present frame of mind, a few signs that Tamsin was not an absolute model of sanctity. The way she had induced him to climb Wilfred's Tower, for instance.

Tamsin had no illusions about herself. "I am not especially good. I'm more frightened of temptation than most girls, that's all. As long as I can remember, I've been determined not to risk the same fate as my mother."

"How old were you when she died?"

"A little above nine years."

She sat down opposite him on a stool, her face young and pale above the enshrouding cloak. It did not occur to either of them how odd this was: that she should be willing to stay in the same room, unprotected, with the young man who had intended to make her his mistress by force. That was over now, irrelevant. What had actually been violated was the surface of certain memories and emotions which were generally dormant. They had to be released in words, so that she was soon saying things to him she would never have told anyone otherwise. Things that were basically more private and revealing than a great deal of the pretended intimacy between lovers.

"My mother was Cornish, a Trelawney of Mavagazion; she married an Englishman who took her to London, where she was content enough until she met my father.

From then on they were both bewitched. Seeing him today, it's incredible to think he could once inspire such a passion, yet they were besotted enough to run away together and count the world well lost for love. Which I don't think it was," she added sadly.

"Well lost?"

"No. They loved each other, right to the end, in spite of everything, I've no doubt of that. But they weren't happy. My mother was continually troubled in her conscience; she was disgraced, ignored, unable to mix with people of reputation; even her sisters would only meet her secretly. They wouldn't receive her in their houses. My father fared better — a man can survive almost any scandal, provided he is well-born and fairly thick-skinned — but it made her angry and bitter if he met his old friends in places where she was no longer welcome, so after a while he cut himself off, and then, because he couldn't spend his whole life shut up with one woman, he began to drink in taverns and frequent low company. And she didn't like that either.

"I dare say she was a fool, she should have reckoned the price she would have to pay for her pleasure. The fact is, no one who hasn't tried it can guess what it feels like to be an outcast. I've known all my life: the sense of being whispered about and stared at, and made to feel inferior without knowing why. The children who weren't allowed to play with me, or worse still, the children who became my dearest companions until sooner or later their parents discovered the truth, and after that I must never go near them again. It was very hard to understand what I'd done wrong. The first time one of our maids told me I was a child of sin, I was terrified. I thought I was going to sprout horns."

"It's outrageous that you should be punished for what your parents had done."

"Outrageous but inevitable. That's one reason I am resolved never to conceive a child out of wedlock. I never want to endure the pangs my mother suffered on my behalf as well as her own. There was one particular time, I was seven, and we were lodging in a village near

London. As long as my father was with us, we were treated with some measure of civility, but he went off on one of his sorties to the City, and I think there must have been a rumour that he had deserted us. When Sunday came round, my mother took me to church; we went every week, though of course she could never receive the Sacrament. After the second lesson, the parson declared that one of the congregation was to be publicly rebuked for her vicious and wicked life. Then he ordered my mother to come out of our pew and face the rows of gaping parishioners, and he kept her there for ten whole minutes while he abused and denounced her as though she wasn't a woman with a soul at all, just a copulating animal. And she had to stand there, weeping and half dead with shame while I hid under the seat and bawled myself into a fever because he said my mother would go to hell."

"But that is horrible," said John. "Vile. How can Christians be so lost to compassion?"

The whole story had shaken him to the depths of his nature, and he felt a curiously personal guilt, as though he was responsible for the anguish of the young woman who had been brutally stripped of all her human dignity, as though he had permanently maimed the lonely little girl who had cried under the pew.

Because he was a man, a rich man who lived safe and untouchable in a country which would grant him every respect while persecuting the women he was only too ready to seduce.

Tamsin seemed to be engrossed in her memories. Hesitant, he asked her, "What happened afterwards?"

"We crept home together as best we could, we hardly knew where we were going. When we got indoors, my mother threw herself on the ground and hid her face; she wouldn't move or speak. I lay beside her and felt her shivering. We didn't have any dinner, I remember. Until the cook came and brought me some broth, and persuaded my mother to go to bed. She was a kind creature.

"Next day, when my father came back, he was furiously enraged against that unmerciful parson; he and his friends went along and broke every window in the vicarage — after which it seemed wiser to pack and leave the district immediately. I suppose he thought he had avenged my mother in some way. It didn't make any difference to her. She never went into a church again."

"I'm not surprised."

"Oh, she bore no malice, she accepted what they had done to her as a judgment on the life she was leading. But still she couldn't bring herself to leave my father. And that is what I find so very hard. I don't believe she stayed with him out of lust or pleasure-seeking, or even out of love; she did love him, but she was heartily sick of wandering in the wilderness, and her health had begun to fail. She stayed with him simply because there was nowhere else that she and I could go. That is how the world and the Church combine against a woman who commits her particular sin. They leave her shut in a trap, and then condemn her because she doesn't get out."

"And that is the trap into which I was trying to entice you."

She looked across at him as though she

was studying him from a new perspective. "I don't suppose you deliberately plotted my ruin."

"That's no justification, is it? I know perfectly well what happens to girls who get pregnant, but I didn't wish to think of it. I didn't wish to think that you were virtuous, either. So I treated you like a harlot. Tamsin, I have nothing to say in my defence. Nothing to offer you but my deep and lasting regret. I hope in time you will be able to forgive me. I don't think I shall ever forgive myself."

"You will find it easier than you imagine," she said cynically. All of a sudden she was worn out. "Will you go now, my lord."

He stood up. It was difficult to know how to end this fantastic encounter, or what the consequence was going to be. He could not plead with her to let him off lightly, not because he was too proud, but because he had refused to listen to her pleading, and he didn't deserve to be let off. Still, he might as well be prepared for the worst that was to come.

"May I know, if you have decided yet, what you are going to do?"

"I don't understand you . . . What should I do?"

"By rights you ought to tell your father how I came here this evening; no doubt he will complain to my guardian — "

"But I thought you wanted me to forgive you? That would be a strange way of setting about it. As it turned out, you did me no harm; what satisfaction should I get from carrying tales to your guardian?"

Not even, she thought, the satisfaction of having him knocked off his lordly pedestal; she had been after something of that sort when she tricked him at Wilfred's Tower. Tonight she had achieved it, single-handed. The insolent, careless amorist who had been selfishly pursuing her for the past few weeks was scarcely recognisable in the utterly humbled and contrite young man who was hoping desperately that she would keep her mouth shut, and too conscience-stricken to ask.

★ ★ ★

During the next ten days it became gradually certain that Tamsin had kept her mouth shut, and that John had nothing to fear in the way of retribution. His relief and gratitude were mixed with an increasing remorse, for the better he thought of her, the worse he thought of himself, of the mean and shallow credulity with which he had accepted the world's version of Tamsin as a public wanton. And no one had misled him more than Bernard and Ann, in spite of all their lofty piety. It was a pity that he could not tell them so.

No one would understand how he felt about Tamsin, he thought as he rode down the avenue one afternoon, alone because he could not bear a lot of chattering people around him. The trouble was, he could not bear too much of his own company either. The same contrariness governed his ride. He had intended to go up on the hill, but now found himself making for Gaultonsbury instead. It was market day, and there was a chance that the Groves might be dining at the White Swan. He was desperately anxious to see Tamsin again, to let her see how sorry he was, in case she had not believed him before. He had tried writing, but it was no use, he could not find the right words. There was very little contact between the two families, and no more weddings or festivities in view at present. The idea of going deliberately to Sutleigh appalled him; how could he pay a civil call at a house he had last entered like a thief? She would probably refuse to meet him. Much better aim for an apparently casual encounter at the inn.

But when he got to the White Swan, the Groves and their usual cronies had none of them been there at all that day.

He stabled his horse, drank a cup of ale, and wandered out into the cobbled Market Place, feeling disconsolate. The market was over, the farmers had driven their beasts away, the good wives had sold their butter and eggs, and all their customers had either gone home or retired into the taverns, so that even the shops were deserted. The shoemaker was putting up his shutters, while the apothecary had sent his apprentice out with a broom to sweep the market flotsam of straw and cabbage-stalks away from his door. The only interesting sight was an old man sitting very dejectedly in the town stocks.

He was a bent and pitiful figure with a wispy beard and looked very uncomfortable pinioned on the ground with his ankles in the wooden sockets. There was something faintly familiar about him; John wondered who he was and what he had done.

Crossing the cobbles, he was astonished to be met by a small, reedy, but perfectly tuneful voice serenading him at knee level: the man in the stocks was keeping up his courage with a song.

"Down in the meadows the other
    day,
A-gathering flowers both fine and gay,
A-gathering flowers both red and blue,
I little thought what love can do."

"Salathiel!" exclaimed John. "That's your name, is it not? You were the ballad-singer at the wedding."

The prisoner looked up. Although he did not recognise the dark young man towering above him, he knew immediately that he was one of the right sort who loved music and feasting in good company — a proper gentleman.

"I've sung at many weddings," he said, "for it is my trade. And no matter when your honour may have seen me, I can tell 'ee I warn't trussed up in the stocks for vagrancy. Never until this day."

"But who took you up? You are no vagrant."

"The parish constable said I was begging. I ask your honour, is it a crime for a man who's been robbed to crave a little meat and bread in a town where he's been known these thirty years and more? I've had nought to eat since daybreak, for those two rogues stole my victuals as well as every penny I had. And they did steal my fiddle . . . " Here poor Salathiel broke down and wept.

"Don't fret," said John gently. "I'll see you have justice, I promise you. Now tell me the whole story."

Salathiel had been travelling the country on foot in his usual way; early this morning, as he crossed the moor, he had been set on by two masterless men, discharged soldiers probably, who had seized all his possessions, including his precious fiddle, and left him penniless. He had tramped on to Gaultonsbury and stopped at the first large house on the edge of the town, because it belonged to Mr. Matthew Webber (a very convivial gentleman, as his honour might know): Unluckily Mr. Webber was out, and while Salathiel was waiting for him to come home, some unspecified killjoy had sent for the constable, complaining that he was a good-for-nothing vagabond, whining for charity.

"Which I han't never done," protested Salathiel, to whom this was a fearful insult. "I do sing for my supper, and I do earn my keep honest, and give good measure."

"To be sure you do. That fool of a constable doesn't know what he's about. I'll go and find him straightway, and get him to set you free."

John had no idea where to look for the constable. He went over to the apothecary's shop to enquire.

While he had been talking to Salathiel, and about a hundred yards along an

145

ancient and narrow passage inevitably called New Street, the doors of the Grammar School had opened to release the scholars who had been mewed up together for six hours, mouthing Latin declensions, and who were aching for any occupation that would stretch their bored minds and cramped bodies. Most of them trooped to a patch of open ground where they could kick a football, but a few strolled along New Street towards the Market Place.

"See what we have here!" Dick Maggs, the butcher's son, glanced round to make sure he had an audience to impress. He was a big, red-faced, beef-fed boy with a strong sense of his own importance "Jem Trotton's found a candidate for the stocks; what do you say we have some sport with him?"

"That's a good notion, Diccon," applauded his familiar, who was sharp and gingery and generally called Foxy.

"We've nothing to throw," objected another boy.

"Yes, we have." Dick scooped up a handful of horse-dung. "We'll have a pelting match. Three shies each, and see

146

who scores most hits."

Their prey, helpless in his wooden trap, gave a bleat of alarm. "I pray you, don't hurt me, young sirs. I never did you no harm."

"Good lord, it's Salathiel!" Simon Grove had just come up behind the others. "You don't want to plague the old fellow, Diccon."

"Why not? He's a rotten ballad-singer." Diccon raised his arm, but Simon caught him by the elbow and the spatter of dung fell wide.

"Stands to reason, he's a friend of Simon's," sniggered Foxy. He added something rude about beggars and bastards and drabs.

Simon flung himself on Foxy.

"Hold on to him!" shouted Diccon to his ally. "Just keep him still, and I'll show Master lousy half-gentleman Grove what he gets for interfering."

John was emerging from the shop on the other side of the Market Place: he saw the whole scene as in a dumbshow. He ran across the square, seized Diccon by his belt, dragged him off his opponent, and gave him a kick in the backside which sent him sprawling on to the cobbles.

"Get up, you dolt!" he said. "Get up and fight fair — if you know how."

Diccon clambered to his feet, gulping with indignation. He turned to deal with the person who had dared to attack him, and found himself confronting a slim popinjay he thought he could floor with one hand. He stumped forward to avenge himself, and was jerked off his balance in the paralysing grip of a wrestler and hurtled back on to the cobbles.

"Next time," said the popinjay pleasantly, "I swear I'll break your arm."

Diccon rubbed his bruises. The other boys had stopped fighting. The crowd of spectators had grown, and through their excited comments came the heavy accent of the law.

"What's the meaning of this affray? I'll have to take you all into custody."

John had at least succeeded in locating the constable.

Determined to avoid side issues, he demanded, "Why did you put that man in the stocks?"

Jem Trotton, the parish constable, was thrown out of his stride. He thought he had come to frighten a rabble of schoolboys, and here was this fully-grown young gentleman slashing back at him in a tone he associated with the more autocratic magistrates.

He glanced sulkily at the prisoner. "The fellow was begging — sir."

"Is it forbidden for a man who has been robbed to ask for succour? Answer me that, will you? And what have you done about the ruffians who assaulted him on the moor? Yes, I know it was outside your parish bounds, but is that any reason why they should escape scot-free? The Justices will send out warrants for them; have you informed Sir Bernard or Mr. Mulcaster?"

Jem Trotton scratched his head. He had arrested Salathiel for begging within the parish of Gaultonsbury; that was what the law said he had to do. Now it was being suggested that he ought to have paid attention to tales about a crime committed somewhere outside his own little territory, but this was too revolutionary; by the time he had been called a sluggard, an imbecile and a cockroach (all epithets that the onlookers very much enjoyed) the constable was quite ready to let Salathiel out of the stocks, if only this sharp tongued young gentleman would go away and leave him in peace.

By now Dick and Foxy had very sensibly taken themselves off, so John was able to attend to the boy who had tried to protect Salathiel; he was concerned to find him sitting on the ground with blood pouring down his face in a most alarming way.

"I fear you've got an ugly cut there. Will you let me see?"

"It's by dose," said Simon, speaking with difficulty. It was, in fact, nothing but a nose-bleed, though John could hardly believe this. He had never seen such quantities of very red and sticky blood. Half a dozen people had produced cloths or kerchiefs to try and staunch the flow, but all the boy could do was soak through one and reach for another. The apothecary brought cold compresses and a basin. Some kindly stranger brought a cushion from the inn. The landlord promptly came out to fetch it back, and then felt he could hardly be so inhuman, with young Master Grove from Sutleigh white as a sheet and weltering in his gore, while Lord Harcourt knelt so anxiously beside him, oblivious of the dirt and the crowd.

A new arrival had followed the landlord through the doorway of the inn. Tamsin and her father had been out to dinner; on the way home they had stopped at the White Swan, stabled their horses and come in through the back entrance. When Tamsin discovered that something extraordinary was happening at the front, she must of course find out what it was.

The sight in the Market Place brought her up short. She stood still, icy cold, and too shocked to think clearly, but aware of horrifying implications — her brother, her would-be seducer, and all that blood.

"Simon!" she exclaimed, and then, before she could bite back the words, "My lord, what have you done to him?"

John looked up, aghast. There was the girl who had been haunting his conscience for a week, more beautiful and accusing than ever, with her soft, vibrant voice, her eyes full of passionate reproach. He had not even realised till now that the schoolboy was her half-brother but he guessed at once what she must be thinking, and what a villain he must look, dishevelled and hatless, with Simon's blood all over his hands. And worst of all, he was completely tongue-tied and could think of nothing to say.

It was Simon who answered Tamsin. "Don't be a fool," he said crossly. "His lordship was on my side."

Bates, the apothecary, said, "His lordship went to Master Simon's aid in a schoolboys' battle, madam. It was all on account of Salathiel being put in the stocks."

"Salathiel?" repeated Tamsin, quite lost. She glanced distractedly towards the stocks, where the constable was helping Salathiel, who was making uncommonly heavy weather about his aches and pains. She did not understand what was going on, but she gathered that John had played a heroic part and that she had reason to be grateful to him. If only she hadn't been so stupid. Perhaps he hadn't heard? It was a vain hope and she knew it.

"That was a splendid throw, the way you tackled Diccon," Simon said to John. The bleeding had eased off a little and he wanted to talk. "I didn't know you could wrestle, sir."

"And your sister thinks I can't shoot; what a lily-fingered creature you both take me for." John got to his feet. He was feeling a good deal better since he had noticed Tamsin's confusion.

The improvement did not last. A party of horsemen had come into the Market Place. Their leader surveyed the populace and was not impressed by what he saw.

"Who the devil started this uproar?" he asked in a voice that John knew only too well.

Plenty of people wanted to tell him. John was not among them; he was too busy retrieving his hat, brushing himself down, and reflecting that ever since he could remember Bernard had shown a genius for turning up at awkward moments.

Dismounting in a leisurely manner, Bernard said, "I can still see no reason why you should all behave as though you had come to watch a bear-baiting. Mrs. Grove, I am sure your brother ought to be indoors. And so, my lord, ought you," he added, grasping John's arm and propelling him firmly towards the inn.

"It is an astonishing matter," he said in an undertone, "that I cannot trust you alone for a couple of hours without you get into some sort of trouble."

John pretended not to hear, ducking his head under a low lintel as they stepped into a rather cheerless parlour with small windows and dark, smoky beams. There was a good deal of coming and going: Tamsin and the apothecary brought Simon in and made him to lie down on the settle. Tom Grove arrived and had to be told the whole history over again; mercifully, he seemed to be sober. The host and his wife kept popping in and out with flagons of wine, clean towels in case poor Master Simon needed them, and encouraging reports about Salathiel who was being given his dinner in the kitchen.

Bernard stood with his back to the empty hearth, one foot tapping impatiently.

When at last they were left alone with the three Groves, John wondered anxiously whether he would consider this private enough for some of the things he was obviously burning to say.

But it was Tom Grove who began, rather unluckily, to admonish his son for his wild behaviour — what did he mean by kicking up such a dust and involving his lordship in a vulgar brawl?

"I suppose I should have just stood back and left old Salathiel to his fate?" muttered Simon. John had every sympathy for him.

"It's high time you learnt to distinguish," he told the boy. "A gentleman is bound to succour the weak and defend all victims of oppression — provided he does it decently on a battlefield in some foreign country. Chivalry towards one of the common people in a public street, that is inexpressibly vulgar."

"Harcourt!" said Bernard sharply.

"Well, sir? Haven't I stated the case?"

As well be hung for a sheep as a lamb, he thought, but he had actually earned his own reprieve, because Bernard was honest enough to recognise some justice

155

in what he had said.

He turned to his neighbour. "I don't think we can blame these young men too harshly for obeying a charitable impulse. Their motives were good."

Grove agreed thankfully (he was not really in his element as a stern parent) and Simon glowed with pride at being described as 'these young men' in conjunction with Lord Harcourt, who had suddenly become his idol.

The constable bustled into the room, eager to save his credit with a show of energy.

"Will it please your lordship to lodge a complaint against those varlets that were disturbing of the peace with their impudent goings-on — "

"Certainly not," said John promptly. "I don't know their names, and I have forgotten what they looked like. And so has Master Simon."

"That's all very well," objected his guardian, "but the proper rules of conduct must be observed: we can't have schoolboys going round assaulting members of the nobility."

"Nobody assaulted me, sir. I assaulted

one of them. I could not possibly bring a charge against him."

"I suppose it does not matter," remarked Tamsin, "what damage they might have done to Simon or Salathiel, so long as they didn't hurt your lordship?"

She was trying to clean up her brother with a damp towel, and sounded decidedly pugnacious.

Turning in her direction but managing not to look at her, John said, "I was thinking chiefly of your brother, Mrs. Grove. If those two barbarians were brought to book, what do you think the outcome would be? The whole Grammar School would decide that Simon had no need to fight fair, because his powerful friends could always settle his quarrels for him. And from then on his life would be made a misery."

"And that's the truth!" agreed Simon with vigour. "Though I can't imagine how you guessed."

John smiled at him. "I didn't have to guess; I know. I wasn't much older than you are when I went up to Oxford."

It struck Tamsin for the first time that John must often find his rank a complication, if not a disadvantage, which perhaps excused some of his mistakes. It also struck her that she had behaved very shabbily to him this afternoon, and she could not think how to put this right, especially as he was now ostentatiously ignoring her.

Her father, Sir Bernard and the constable had become engrossed in a discussion about catching the two footpads.

After a moment John observed to the room at large, "I think I'll have a word with Salathiel. I want to buy him a new fiddle."

Tamsin watched him go with an agony of confused sensations. Then she came to a decision. She slipped out after him.

As she closed the door behind her, he was on the point of disappearing through an archway at the end of the short passage.

"My lord."

He stopped, without turning round. "Yes?"

"My lord, if I might speak with you for a minute, there is something I want — I ought to say to you."

He came back to her, very stiff and grave.

"I want to thank you for going to my brother's rescue. I am indeed grateful. Only I fear I haven't shown it very well. When I first saw you together, I thought — "

"I understood perfectly what you thought."

She braced herself to continue. There was something else she had to say, it had been weighing on her mind for the past week. "That night when I allowed you to take all the blame, I know very well that it was partly my fault. I had let you think I was the sort of woman who — in short, I did lead you on."

"Yes," he said, quite gently. "Do you mind telling me why?"

She was staring straight ahead of her, transfixed by the stripes of his green and white doublet. She knew the honest answer to that question. Having denied herself the pleasure of casual love-making, she had to find some way of amusing herself. It was not pretty. Of course there had been other reasons.

"I was trying to teach you a lesson."

"You succeeded in teaching us both a lesson."

"Yes." She took a deep breath. "I am well aware what names there are to describe the way I have behaved towards you."

"But I hope you know I would never dream of using them," he assured her, and she noticed what a deep and beautiful voice he had.

She glanced up, a little uncertainly, and John for his part wondered how he could ever have taken her for a hardened wanton. He could tell now how innocent and vulnerable she was, in spite of all her gallant pretending.

One of the tapsters came up the cellar stairs at the end of the passage, carrying a large jug of ale. They heard him go into the common parlour, and the wave of laughter and roistering that surged out to meet him. It became essential to break their own spell of silence.

"How is your mare?" she asked at random. "Your little Barb. I hope she was none the worse; I didn't let her go till we were nearly back at Minton."

"Oh, she's in fine fettle. I am training

her in the art of Manage; I exercise her every morning on that flat piece of ground beside the North Wood."

Normally Tamsin would have viewed this gambit with immediate suspicion, but today she merely replied that she often went that way to visit their old woodcutter's wife.

After which they each wondered vaguely, why did I say that?

It was a fair comment on their state of mind that neither of them knew.

★ ★ ★

Two mornings later Tamsin happened to be walking round the edge of North Wood just when John happened to be exercising his little Barb in one of the more spectacular feats of the Manage: galloping her in full career, and then suddenly checking her back on her quarters to make an almost spiral turn. It was a magnificent sight — the young man dressed in scarlet on the rearing horse, rampant against a green field. Any poet could have said that John Harcourt rode like a Centaur.

When he saw Tamsin, he took off his feathered hat with a flourish; she raised her hand in acknowledgement and went steadfastly on, her hooped skirt swinging to the rhythm of her footsteps as she brushed across the dewy grass. Neither of them spoke.

On her return journey, he was still there. He had dismounted, and was carefully feeling the mare's fetlocks. Leading her, he came over to talk to Tamsin, and was given an elaborate account of the old woodcutter's wife, sick of the palsy and needing so much attention.

Next day she found it necessary to visit the old woman again, but she did not bother to produce an explanation when John immediately got down and came to walk along beside her for about half a mile.

After that they met frequently. There were no definite assignations, but each took care to find out where the other was going, so that neither could pretend to be surprised when John, climbing down over the summit of the ridge from the Minton side, came upon Tamsin sitting in a nest of bracken on the green slope above Sutleigh. Or when Tamsin rode into his combe for a change, and discovered John watering his horse on the opposite bank of the Minton stream.

When they met, they talked. Nothing more. He did not attempt to make love to her. Nowadays he treated her with a punctilious respect, and she felt safe with him in the loneliest places. They learnt a great deal about each other in these long, dawdling hours together, and if they had both begun to reach some rather unsettling conclusions, they were wise enough to keep these hidden, and to go on talking about every subject under the sun.

One afternoon, towards the end of May, they were in their little scooped-out hollow above Sutleigh village, sitting on a trampled carpet of last autumn's dead bracken, and screened by the new green fronds that were forcing their way through to the light. Below them lay the small enclosures where Mr. Mulcaster had planted oats and hemp and flax inside thickset hedges of apples and pears, now crested with pale blossom.

Surrounding these enclosures lay the open champaign fields that were shared out between the whole community, each man getting his own few rows to sow. Tiny figures could be seen weeding and hoeing, or plodding laboriously along the narrow grass paths between the corn.

"Poor creatures, how hard they have to toil," remarked John. "And all for such a small gain. They look like ants from up here."

"I fancy they generally look like ants to your lordship."

He gave her a sideways glance, flushing a little. "You know just how to put me in my place, don't you? What an arrogant monster I must appear to you."

"My dear lord, you are mistaken, I assure you!"

She was honestly sorry, for she had meant only to tease him, not expecting him to be so vulnerable.

She held out her hand to him in an impulsive gesture of friendliness. He took it, and they both received a tremor of warning, too late. The two dark pairs of eyes searched each other for a moment, then he lifted her hand and kissed the inside of the palm, near where the blue veins came in at the wrist.

Tamsin snatched back her hand. "Why can't you leave me alone?" she almost shouted at him in a mixture of anger and entreaty. "Why do you have to plague me? Oh God, I might have known how it would be!"

"Tamsin, I didn't intend to do that. I swear to you it wasn't deliberately planned."

She had clambered to her feet, not an easy thing to do gracefully in the deep bracken. In a low, cold voice she said, "Will your lordship be pleased to let me pass."

"In a minute, if you must. First let me explain — "

"What good will that do? This is the end. I can't go on meeting you now."

"For heaven's sake, why not?" He studied as much as he could see of the implacable profile that was turned away from him. "All I did was to kiss your hand. I'm not back at my old games, I promise you. Don't you trust me?"

"How can I?" she whispered. "How

can I trust you not to take advantage of my weakness?"

"Tamsin, I'll do no such thing!" he burst out in real distress. "Whatever I may have done in the past, surely you know I'd never hurt you now? I'd never dream of making love to you without your consent."

Tamsin did not ask what he would do if he got her consent. No sense in pointing out the real weakness which was rapidly becoming plain to her.

John tried again. "Don't turn away from me. I love you so very much — "

"You must not say that. The only kind of love which could ever exist between us would be a deadly sin."

"That's not true." He saw her preparing to flash back at him in a blaze of righteous scorn, and got his word in first. "There would be nothing sinful in my loving you if we were married."

This startled Tamsin enough to silence her for a minute. Then she said crossly, "Don't be a fool."

"You aren't very civil." He was laughing now, buoyed up by a sudden excitement and gaiety, because he had

166

just deduced the answer to a question that had been tormenting him for the past fortnight. "I'm making you an honourable offer of marriage; a little unpolished, it's true, for I've not had much practice. Still, it was unkind of you to call me a fool."

She stared at him, unbelieving. "Harcourt, how could we marry, even supposing you — supposing we both wished it? We are under age. Your friends would never allow it."

John had a vivid mental picture of himself explaining the matter to Bernard. He said, regretfully, "I'm afraid we should have to keep the marriage a secret for the time being. Live apart with our own families, I mean, and seize on what opportunities we could get. It wouldn't be for very long."

"What if I had a child?"

"Then we could admit the truth and our troubles would be over. For you see how it is, sweetheart: if my cousin found us out directly after the marriage, I think he might try to get it disallowed on some legal quibble, and though he couldn't accomplish much so long as we both stood firm, he could probably keep us apart and make life intolerable until my coming-of-age. But suppose we were able to say that you were expecting a child, undoubtedly conceived in wedlock, then Bernard would be forced to accept you with a good grace. He'd never risk any action that might cast doubts on the legitimacy of my heir."

Tamsin thought this over. It seemed quite sound, if not very agreeable. She was disturbed to find herself contemplating a deceitful private contract with a young man of nineteen whose station was so immeasurably far above hers that her own pride ought to forbid such an unequal match. Yet if John didn't mind the disparities, why should she be so scrupulous?

"Are you persuaded that you know what you are suggesting? I won't speak of my lack of a dowry, for I daresay that means little to a man of your wealth, but there is the misfortune of my birth, and people will tell stories about me — "

He didn't care a straw about any of those old slanders, he interrupted her fiercely. He loved her, he trusted her, he wanted to rescue her from the slights and insults she had suffered for so long, and give her a home where she would be happy and cherished for ever.

"That's all very well," she commented rather dampeningly, "but who would perform the ceremony? I fear we should get short shrift from the Vicar."

Neither of the vicars of their adjoining parishes would dream of marrying them without the approval of both their guardians, while the household chaplain at Minton would be even less anxious to incur the patron's wrath. She half expected John's enthusiasm to founder on this rock, and wondered whether it was going to divert him towards another solution: if we exchange vows and rings it will come to the same in the end. Once we are betrothed; there's no need to wait for the wedding . . . He would not be the first man who had told her this fairy-tale.

He astounded her by producing quite a different answer. "It's not so hard as you think. There are always clergymen willing to conduct a secret marriage for the sake of the fee. Poor fellows who can't get preferment because they've been too outspoken, perhaps. Or too hair-splitting in their theology. I know of a man who would be able to settle the business for us, though it might take a week or so to get him here. What do you say, my dear life? If I can lay hold of a parson, will you come to the wedding?"

"I don't know, I must have more time to consider — " She was ashamed of having doubted him, and this added to her confusion. The situation was too unexpected. "I need the chance to examine my own feelings — "

"That's a subject we can explore together," said John promptly.

What he taught her about her feelings during the next few minutes confirmed all her suspicions. The pleasure that stole over her as he kissed her was so acute it almost frightened her. Perpetually on her guard, she had never allowed herself to be so responsive to any man before; presently she began to feel they ought to call a halt, but while she was still trying to summon the will-power, he very gently released her, saying that they must take care not to do anything for which their consciences might later reproach them.

This, coming from John, left her speechless. At least she was finally convinced that he did want to marry her.

June

TAMSIN spent the morning of her wedding-day turning out the linen chest, unable to believe in the climax towards which this dull, ordinary day was carrying her. She kept slipping her hand inside her bodice to touch the stiff folds of John's letter, in which he told her that he had got hold of an obliging clergyman, and also that he had arranged to spend a night away from Minton by inventing a visit to the Maltbys at Chilcote.

Tamsin had told her father casually that she would be staying at Abbotsleat to help Mrs. Mulcaster prepare for the sheep-shearing feast next week. She set off after dinner, but not to Abbotsleat. She circled round the village so that she could approach the church discreetly from the back. As she was tethering the little grey gelding to an iron ring in the churchyard wall, Giles Brown appeared and asked anxiously whether she thought that was safe. They had hidden the other horses some way off, not wishing to draw attention to what they were doing in the church. He spoke as though it was something rather disgraceful.

"Anyone who sees Grey Vanity will have to imagine I am saying my prayers," retorted Tamsin.

She stepped on to the low wall and jumped down among the graves, ignoring the arm Giles held out to her. It struck her that he did not like this marriage, perhaps none of John's servants could be expected to like it — which was a bleak thought.

Then John himself appeared between the yew-trees, and she forgot everything except the happiness of being close to him again, and the laughter and confidence in his eyes as he greeted her.

"I see you've done as I requested you," he murmured, looking at the way her thick, dark hair was brushed over her shoulders.

"Oh, was that a request? I mistook it for a command."

John had insisted that she was to be married 'in her hair' as a young virgin ought to be, although Tamsin said that this would look odd to anyone who saw her riding about the combe; at eighteen she wore her hair pinned up as a rule, and only let it hang loose on formal or festive occasions. But she was glad she had given in, if the symbolism meant so much to him.

The clergyman came forward now, and John presented him.

"This is Mr. Blake, my love, who has come a long way to give us our hearts' desire, so we have good cause to be grateful to him."

Mr. Blake was an impressively tall, austere cleric, dressed all in black, with white hair and fine, regular features. He greeted her formally; his resonant tones would have filled a cathedral.

They went into the porch, and here she was confronted by another stranger: a man in a very tawdry salmon-pink doublet, embroidered with tarnished silver thread and badly frayed at the cuffs. He looked thoroughly out of place in the doorway of Sutleigh church, and seemed well aware of it, for above his waxed moustaches a pair of pale eyes were nervously beseeching. John said that this was Mr. Munday; he and Giles were going to act as their witnesses.

She had forgotten that they would need two witnesses. Mr. Munday bowed over her hand with excruciating servility, and they all went inside the church.

It was quite unlike the morning she had come there as one of Charity Mulcaster's bridesmaids. She had assured herself that she would not mind having a different sort of wedding from other girls, and now she actually found that this was true. She did not want the critical whispering crowds, and all the junketing over ribbons and garters. She much preferred the simplicity of the empty building, the shell of holy silence which contained Mr. Blake's reading of the Marriage Service and the deep voice of her bridegroom, broken by a faint tremor, as he said: "I, John, take thee, Thomasine, to my wedded wife . . . "

It was soon over, and they were out in the sunshine. Tamsin was lost in a cloud of unreality while the horses were reclaimed; Giles rode off in a great hurry — but apparently they were going to meet him later. The parson and Mr. Munday bid them a respectful goodbye and vanished in the opposite direction.

Tamsin was so intrigued by them that the first thing she did when left alone with her husband was to ask him, "What's the matter with Mr. Blake?"

John was tightening Vanity's girths for her; he paused without lifting his head. "What should be the matter with him? Were you not satisfied with the manner in which he conducted the service?"

"On the contrary. No one could have done it more reverently. But to come here and marry us, in another man's parish, and without a licence or the calling of banns — you told me yourself that the kind of parson who will agree to such devices is generally in some difficulty, and I wondered what Mr. Blake's troubles could be. He looks like an archdeacon, though it seems strange he should consort with such a man as Munday."

"As to that, it's no concern of ours. I believe that Munday owes a great deal to him," said John a little sententiously, adding that Blake did not find himself able to hold a living at the present time.

He turned his attention to his own horse, the big black Nero, put his hand on the pummel and vaulted into the saddle with an athletic grace that was no less notable because it was calculated. They set off in high spirits.

"Don't you want to know where I am taking you?"

She had been puzzling about this ever since he had promised that they should spend their wedding night in undisturbed privacy. They were heading straight up the combe and into the wilderness, where there were very few houses at all.

"I hope we're not going to Wilfred's Tower?"

"It would serve you right if we were. But it's another tall building, on an even higher hill. Can't you guess?"

She thought for a moment, gazing up at the high ridges that rolled above them. "John — how clever of you! We're going to your cousin's hunting-lodge."

Sir Bernard had built himself a convenient lodge, right at the heart of the deer-forest, with a view over the whole terrain, where he and his friends could stay when they came up in the late summer and autumn to hunt the hart at force. Most of the year it stood idle with one of the verderers and his family living there to keep the place aired and dry. John had bribed the caretakers to let him borrow the lodge for the night; Giles and one of his grooms had gone on there now to make the final preparations.

They rode on up, along the tracks that ran between the thickets of gorse and bracken. They did not talk much. At one moment it seemed good to them to sing the whole of Sweet Nightingale through from beginning to end, because the last verse was so appropriate.

The couple agreed, and were married
  with speed,
And soon to the church they did go.
No more's she afraid for to walk in
  the shade,
Nor sit in those valleys below,
Nor sit in those valleys below.

For that was the triumphant conclusion of all such songs: the delights which the man offered and the girl refused were to be enjoyed at last within the boundaries of marriage. They glanced at each other, and each had their secret thoughts. Not very long now.

When they reached the hunting-lodge, Giles came out to meet them, and John's groom led the horses away. The lodge stood on a hilltop, tall and narrow, with the evening light glittering on the windows. There was a strange, fairy-tale isolation about it, and there did not seem to be a soul there except themselves.

They climbed to a vast chamber which occupied the whole of the third floor, and which was their entire domain until tomorrow morning. It looked a little peculiar, because the lodge was practically unfurnished, except during the hunting season, and Giles had been able to smuggle only small, portable things from Minton. There were no curtains, no wall-hangings, and no rushes on the floor, the boards were bare. There was a bed in one corner, with a carved oak canopy; it had been made up, but the hangings were missing. On the other side of the room, however, there was a table set with a cold collation of stuffed capon with a raised veal pie, and a salad of lettuce and marigolds, as well as jellies and dishes of comfits, and all sorts of little savoury kickshaws. The table was elegantly set out with silver plate, and there were plenty of candles, all in silver sconces, and other small attempts at luxury — bright silk cushions, a looking-glass of polished steel, and most touching of all, a big bowl of carnations, the ragged sort called sops-in-wine, obviously imported from the garden at Minton; their sweetness scented the air.

"Well, it's better than I thought it would be," said John. "Not a palace, I'm afraid, sweetheart. Can you contrive to make do with it?"

Tamsin assured him that she could. In her present mood she would have spent the night in the ruins of Wilfred's Tower if John had asked her to.

Giles said in a disparaging way that it was damp and draughty, he couldn't get that woman to sweep properly, and no one had brought up the wine. He went clattering downstairs again, sounding very cross.

"Poor Giles," said Tamsin. "I fear he is displeased about the wedding."

"What makes you say that, my treasure?" enquired John, in the intervals of kissing her.

"Why else should he be so out of humour? He thinks I am not good enough for you."

She could have bitten out her tongue a moment afterwards, for when his faithful henchman came back into the room carrying two bottles of wine, John immediately challenged him.

"Giles!"

"My lord?"

"Lady Harcourt thinks you don't approve of her. Would you kindly explain to her that it is I who am suffering under the bane of your disapproval."

"Oh no!" protested Tamsin, her embarrassment slightly mitigated by the pleasure of hearing John call her Lady Harcourt in such a matter-of-fact way.

Staring stolidly in front of him, Giles said, "I am sure you both know very well that it is not for me to pass judgment on either of you."

John took a deep breath. "You are

181

confoundedly stiff-necked, aren't you? What more must I do to allay your scruples? I suppose I must tell her ladyship myself. The fact is, sweetheart, Giles says I ought not to have brought you here."

"Why not?"

"On account of the caretaker being in my cousin's service, and the deep water he'd be in if it was found out what use we'd make of the lodge. The Penellums are all downstairs in their quarters now, pretending not to know that you have arrived. That's why there is no maidservant to wait on you, which is very unfitting."

"I don't care a fig for that, but I should be sorry to bring down your cousin's wrath on the caretaker." Another thought struck her. "You say they are pretending, but of course they *do* know. No doubt they peeped out and recognised me. How can we be sure they won't talk?"

"Why, for the reason I gave you. They would be putting their own heads in the noose."

"Yes," she said, still doubtful. Fear and cupidity would shut most mouths, but there were some morsels of news so choice and rare that no woman, at any rate, could resist the excited self-importance of passing them on. "If you think that Nancy Penellum won't be tempted to tell all her gossips that we are married — " She broke off, as her companions exchanged glances. So that was it. How stupid not to have guessed. "I'm talking nonsense, aren't I? They've heard nothing of any wedding. They simply believe that you brought me here for — for a night's adventure, is it not so? And that kind of news, concerning either you or me, my lord, has too little spice of novelty to make it worth repeating."

This was meant to strike a note of witty unconcern. It failed lamentably. She merely sounded hurt and forlorn, choking back the tears in her throat.

John said: "Be damned to you, Giles — you were absolutely right. I ought to have known better."

He walked across the room and stood with his back to them, gazing out of one of the high windows. Presently he spoke to Tamsin over his shoulder.

"I didn't mean to expose you to yet more slanders. I'm supposed to be the guardian of your reputation — and I'm not indifferent to such matters, I beg you not to think that. I wanted you to be so happy here, and now you are angry, and everything is spoilt."

"No, it's not!" Tamsin ran to put her arms round him, urgently persuading. "My darling, my sweet, honey lord, I swear I'm not angry. It was foolish of me, I should have considered: how could we avoid this deceit? If you acknowledged me as your wife anywhere within a day's ride of Minton, your cousin would be certain to hear of it. So why should we court discovery? It doesn't matter what anyone thinks, so long as we two know that in God's sight we are married."

"You are far too generous," he said with a slow wonder. "I don't deserve it. Tamsin, forgive me."

"For what?" They were alone now; she had heard Giles slip out and close the door.

"For the wrongs I have done you in the past. And for the future; I may need much more forgiving. I haven't lived as I should, I'm not fit to touch you, and if you knew what a wretched creature I am, you would never have consented to this scheme. You wouldn't have trusted me."

"Dear John, I have consented. I have trusted you, so it's too late for ifs and buts."

This was meant to distract him, which it did. He came back from his inward doubts, his regret for a lost innocence, to a present moment that existed solely for one over-mastering purpose.

It was after midnight when they finally ate their wedding-breakfast, sitting up in bed, having at last noticed that they were hungry. John went to fetch some of the dishes from the table, but they never used the candles, there was enough light without them. Each of the four walls had an enormous window, the windows were uncurtained; the moonlight came streaming in, pouring over the bed. Their bodies were turned to silver, etched with shadows of the leaded panes that crisscrossed on their bare skin, so that they were transformed and looked like the splendid pagan royalty of some mythical country under the sea.

Later, when she was on the delicious borders of sleep, Tamsin heard herself say: "If I'd known . . . how glorious it would be . . . I'd never have held out so long."

She was dimly conscious that this was not a proper sentiment for a bride on her wedding-night. She tried to open her eyelids.

"Did I say that aloud?"

"Yes, my sweet, you did. And I feel constrained to tell you that I think it highly reprehensible."

But Tamsin had fallen asleep. John leant on his elbow, watching her and smiling. He allowed her to rest for a short while before he woke her again.

July

THE house at Minton Gabriel was full of visitors, people from the great world who were glad to get away to the country at this season, now that the Queen was off on one of her progresses, and London made very disagreeable by the stinking river and the fear of plague.

One afternoon when Tamsin was walking home from the village, she came across a capsized coach completely filling the lane. Two wheels were in the ditch, two more were pointing towards the sky, and the horses, just released from the shafts, were milling about in confusion while the grooms and coachmen tried to disentangle their reins, not much helped by the orders of two gentlemen who kept contradicting each other.

High and dry on the opposite bank, like shipwrecked mariners, were a handsome middle-aged lady in very fine plumage, two meek attendants, and the prettiest fair-haired, blue-eyed girl Tamsin had ever seen.

She went across to the lady and asked if she could be of any assistance. She was caught in a bright, discontented gaze that was at the same time wryly amused.

"Are you able to put that carriage back on its legs again, mend a broken shaft, cure my maid of coach-sickness, and my husband of a confoundedly bad temper, besides procuring for me a feather bed in a darkened chamber and twelve hours of seclusion? No, I thought not. Then there is very little other service you can render me."

Tamsin smiled. "I fear I am a poor sort of sorcerer, madam. I could, however, direct one of your servants where to find the village carpenter."

"Well, that will be a start. Alexander! This — this young gentlewoman knows where you can get a carpenter."

The slight hesitation was not lost on Tamsin. Who on earth, the lady was visibly wondering, could this apparition be? She had the dress and manner of a person of breeding, yet here she was, on foot and unattended on the Queen's highway. The vicar's daughter? Tamsin did not look like a vicar's daughter.

The man called Alexander seemed anxious to hear about the carpenter. His companion had other ideas.

"I should feel happier if we could escort her ladyship and Lucy to their journey's end. It can't be far now." He addressed himself rather imperiously to Tamsin. "Be so good as to tell me how much longer must we continue on this road before we come to Sir Bernard Kettering's house at Minton Gabriel?"

"For another eight hours, I should imagine," retorted Tamsin. And before the imperious gentleman had time to explode, she said meekly, "You will get there much faster if you turn round. You are in the wrong combe. This is Sutleigh, not Minton."

Alexander let out a hoot of malicious laughter. "Well, if that doesn't set the seal on it! What a marvellous traveller you are, Robert. Cross Arabia Deserta and then get lost in the wilds of Somerset!"

Tamsin had now identified the party. The man accused of losing the way was Sir Robert Evesham, the famous explorer who had been all over Southern Europe and into some parts of Asia; she had heard a great deal about him, for he was a very bright star in John's firmament of heroes. The other people were Mr. Alexander Howard, his wife Lady Dorothy, and their daughter Lucy. John had told her about them all, though not so much, perhaps, about Lucy. He had never said how pretty she was.

Evesham, no longer impervious, was consulting Tamsin about roads and distances when Howard said suddenly: "Sutleigh!"

They all looked at him.

"I knew I'd heard of the place before. Tom Grove of Sutleigh, haven't seen him for years. You must remember Tom Grove, Robert."

"Grove?" Evesham flashed a suddenly enlightened glance at Tamsin. "Well, never mind that now, my dear fellow."

Howard paid no attention. "You can't have forgotten the scandal there was when he ran off with that beautiful Cornish wife of Will Paget's — what was her name? I think she was a Killigrew."

At one time Tamsin would have

suffered this in silence, but recent events had given her the courage to hold her head high.

She said sweetly, "I'm sorry to contradict you, sir. My mother was Julian Trelawney of Mavagazion; she wouldn't have thanked you for calling her a piratical Killigrew."

It was Robert Evesham's turn to laugh.

"You should have heard her put Howard to rout," he informed the company in the long gallery at Minton three hours later. "After which she arranged our deliverance by sending all over the parish to procure enough riding horses for us, and while we waited she entertained us as though the hedgerow was her withdrawing-room. A remarkable young woman. Considering Tom and Julian made such a shambles of their lives, it's a pleasure to know there was one thing they managed supremely well."

It was hateful for John to keep quiet when Tamsin was being discussed, even when the judgment was flattering. Hateful to know that she was excluded from the charmed circle at Minton, though none of the women there could hold a candle to her.

With the connivance of his groom Jenkyn he was now able to ride secretly over to Sutleigh almost every night, returning before daybreak. It was lucky they could manage these nocturnal meetings, for with so much entertainment going on at Minton, John could not escape unnoticed in the daytime as he had in May and June.

So it was a particular pleasure when he manœuvred an afternoon that he could spend with Tamsin; they had arranged to meet at their special place in the bracken where he had asked her to marry him. He was passing through the long gallery on his way out when he was pounced on by Giles.

"I was afraid you'd already started, my lord. Sir Bernard is asking for you."

"What does he want? Not that I wish to know; I'm late, as it is."

"Something damnably awkward. Old Finch took it into his head to get out all your lordship's plate and ornaments, the stuff that was stowed away in those two big chests, so that he could check the inventory. When he found various pieces missing, what must he do but run straight

192

off and complain to the steward."

"For heaven's sake!" said John, disgusted. "Why do I have to put up with such a fool?"

Finch was his groom of the chambers, a self-important, elderly man who deeply resented the unceremonious way his master was living at Minton, and pined for the feudal glories of Laleham and Crossingbourne. He expressed his frustration by ferreting out imagined injuries, and grumbling to the steward on every possible occasion.

"Do go and pacify him," said John. "Pacify them both, or they'll be at each other's throats. By the time I return I've no doubt my missing property will have reappeared exactly where he laid it away, and then he'll have to eat humble-pie."

"You don't understand, my lord. Finch is crying out for the missing pieces of that set of gilt cups and platters with the design of oak-leaves, the ones you told me to sell because you needed the money."

"Good grief, so I did! I'd forgotten that. Back in April, to pay off a gaming debt to Toby Strange. And there was the second time, when I wanted a sweetener for Penellum so that Tamsin and I might lie at the hunting-lodge — "

"Not to speak of the sum you gave to that villain Blake, though why he had to have so much, considering the circumstances — "

"Never mind Blake! We've nothing to fear on that score at present. It's this other business concerns us now; what the devil are we to do?" John pondered for a moment. "You sold that stuff in Garth, didn't you? Not in Gaultonsbury. Then there's a reasonable hope it may not be traced. Provided we keep quiet, no one will ever learn the truth."

He paused. Giles had on that mute and mulish air of disapproval he knew only too well.

"What's the harm in that?" he said defensively. "Oh, I daresay there'll be some sort of inquisition, and the whole place will be searched, but after all they can't discover what isn't here, and there are so many people in this house that I can't see how the dread of being taken for a thief can hang heavily over any one of them. Can you?"

"Yes," said Giles. "Unfortunately there is someone, a young serving man called Turner. He stole a silver ladle from the buttery about a year ago and was found out. Sir Bernard didn't wish to prosecute. He had Turner publicly whipped in front of his fellow-servants, and that was meant to be the end of it. But immediately Finch announced that your lordship had been robbed, you can guess how many fingers were pointed in Turner's direction. And the worst of it is, don't you see, that the more the poor wretch protests his innocence, as he is bound to do, the less they will believe him, and the angrier they will be."

"I suppose they will," said John slowly. "It hadn't struck me there would be anyone so — so vulnerable." This put an entirely different emphasis on the whole matter. He braced himself for what must be done. "I shall have to go to my cousin and tell him the best story I can."

He went downstairs, meeting three different people who said that Sir Bernard was asking for him. He thanked them without enthusiasm.

When he rapped on the library door,

there were so many people talking inside that they did not hear him, so he walked in.

Bernard was sitting judicially at his table, looking exasperated. He was listening to a speech from Finch, who was waving one of the remaining gilt platters that Giles hadn't disposed of. Mr. Creed, the steward, was in attendance, and so were Edmund Royden, the secretary, Zachary Allen, the clerk of the kitchens, and a rabbit-faced individual who was presumably the unhappy Turner.

"It's a wicked slander," Zachary Allen was declaring stoutly. "A wicked slander, Master Finch; trying to pin the blame on a poor lad who once did wrong and suffered his penance for it. What other cause have you to pick on him?"

"He's a known thief, isn't he? Who else is it likely to be?"

"That's what I'm endeavouring to discover," said Bernard crisply. "My lord, I'm very glad to see you. We are in some perplexity here — "

"If I could speak with you privately — "

He was interrupted by Turner, who broke away from Allen and flung himself on his knees, begging John to help him. "I didn't steal from you, my lord, I swear to God I'm innocent, but they mean to put me in prison. They'll burn me in the hand." Fear of the branding iron had reduced him to tears. "Save me, my lord, save me, or they'll burn me in the hand."

"No one is going to hurt you," John told him awkwardly. "There has been a mistake; you have nothing to fear. Do, for heaven's sake get up, man ... As for you, Finch, I don't know what call you had to be so damned interfering, but next time you imagine I've been robbed, you might have the sense to come and tell me so, instead of raising such an infernal hue and cry."

Finch started to protest, but Kettering said sharply: "That's enough! I wish to confer with his lordship. The rest of you have leave to go."

And when they were alone he came straight to the point.

"Well, what's become of the stuff? It's plain you know the answer."

"I sold it."

At least Bernard didn't go into

paroxysms of astonishment. He sat there, even more flint-faced than usual, and merely asked: "Why?"

"For the money."

"Don't be impertinent, Harcourt."

"I'm sorry, sir. I didn't mean to be," said John quite sincerely.

He had realised at the outset what an awkward question this was going to be. If he refused to explain why he needed the money so badly, Bernard would start making investigations which would probably lead him to Tamsin.

Better make an admission that did not involve her directly.

He said: "I had gaming losses."

"Gaming?" repeated Bernard, and it dawned on John, too late, that this was one of the most dangerous things he could have said.

"If anyone in my service has been fleecing you — "

"No," said John quickly. He did not want any more unjust suspicious flying around Minton. "I've never staked more than a few shillings here, I assure you, sir."

"Then who the devil have you been

playing with, and where?" Sir Bernard considered for a moment. The possibilities were decidedly limited; it was not surprising that he hit on the most obvious. "I suppose you have got into the clutches of that precious coven at Sutleigh — Tom Grove's tribe of cheats and vultures. Very well, you don't have to reply; I can see I've guessed right. I might have known you would manage to seek out someone who could pander to your vicious craving for excitement and make a fool of you at the same time. I know you are so weak that you can hardly resist the smallest temptation to any kind of self-indulgence, but I should have thought that even you would have known better than to play cards or hazard with men like Toby Strange and his cronies. What a gold-mine you must have seemed to them! How much more do you owe?"

"Nothing, sir. I have cleared the whole amount."

Long practice had taught him to keep his voice indifferent, and to stand and endure his cousin's most blistering comments with an easy and faintly insolent grace, feet apart and hands clasped loosely behind his back, his uncaring gaze fixed in mid-air a few inches above Bernard's head. It had always been a point of honour to conceal the chasms of guilt and apprehension that Bernard invariably cracked open in the surface of a character which was not nearly so tough as John himself liked to pretend. He had learnt to act this part almost as soon as he had learnt to bear physical pain without crying. By now he did it so well that he generally maddened his guardian into being much harsher than he meant. Bernard had never seen any reason to spare him, and he did not do so this afternoon.

John was told he had been disobedient, dishonest and deceitful. There was also a stern lecture about gambling which missed its target, because in fact John was not a gamester. Of the money Giles had got for him by selling the plate, only a small part had gone to Toby Strange, and that was simply to pay a debt John had acquired while he was hopefully pursuing Tamsin. So he was able to ignore this portion of the homily, staring through the window at the hot, geometric patterns of the flower-beds and the green summer woods, thinking of his darling waiting and waiting for him, wondering why he did not come.

He returned to the consciousness of Bernard saying: "I shall require you to promise me that so long as you are in my charge you will not play for money without my permission, and that you will neither associate with Grove nor enter his house on any pretext whatever."

Warnings of danger prickled up John's spine. The first two promises would cost nothing beyond the annoyance of having to make them. He hadn't the slightest desire to try his luck against Tom Grove or anybody else. The third proviso meant something entirely different. If he promised not to enter Grove's house, how was he to visit Tamsin? He did not know what to do. He tried to slide out of the quandary as best he could.

"Since you think so poorly of me, I don't know why you should trouble to exact a promise. Surely you don't expect me to keep it?"

"That's the first time I have ever heard of a Harcourt boasting he couldn't keep his word. I have often wondered what your ancestors would make of you."

Bernard saw John flush, and acknowledged privately that he was being unjust. In spite of all his caustic remarks, he did really believe in John's essential integrity. Whether he would have the strength to resist any serious temptation, that was a different matter. There had been one Harcourt who had thrown away a thousand pounds in a single night, and another who had lost everything down to his wife's dowry, and finally cut his throat. If the present head of their house had the same sickness in the blood, he had got to be cured of it before he gained control of his fortune. So Bernard ordered him to do what he was told without making any more bones about it.

"I'm sorry, sir. I don't feel able to comply with your wishes."

"Don't you, by God?" said Bernard softly. He studied John for a moment with a very chilling eye. "Very well, then. I shall have to use other means. You will go to Nunehead in the morning, and there you will stay until you have been brought to a more proper frame of mind."

"To Nunehead!" echoed John, very much taken aback.

Nunehead was a small manor separated from the rest of Kettering's property and about seventeen miles from Minton. It was in a most inaccessible place, at the far end of a very long, narrow combe, with a rutty track leading into it, and nothing when you got there but the manor itself, a few cottages and a tiny church. The house was poky and damp, it faced north into the hillside, which was so steep and thickly wooded that the sun never managed to penetrate. It always seemed to be raining at Nunehead.

I won't go, John told himself. I'll tell him so. I've got to assert myself one day, and it's high time I began.

Taking his courage firmly in hand, he said: "I see no cause why I should be packed off to Nunehead, sir, and I may as well tell you that I don't intend to go."

Having made this announcement, he waited for the skies to fall, which in a sense they did, though not quite the way he expected, for Bernard merely said: "You won't be given any choice. If I decided to send you to Nunehead, then that is where you will go, even though it takes six men to carry you."

There was a stupefied pause while John digested this.

"You wouldn't dare!" he said after a moment. "You wouldn't dare to compel me by force. I'll complain to the Court of Wards, and to the Privy Council. I certainly don't wish to exalt my station in front of you, Sir Bernard, but after all I am a peer of England, not a child or a peasant to be bundled about against my will, and I think you are exceeding your authority. I am quite prepared to appeal to the Queen."

"By all means," retorted Bernard. "You may write to Her Majesty from Nunehead; I will supply you with pen and ink, and see that your letter is carried directly by the post. Now, listen to me, Harcourt." He leant forward slightly, his strong features implacable, and the sardonic note in his voice was replaced by a cold contempt. "I do not need to be reminded of your birth and heritage.

I am aware that my right to control you rests solely on the fact that the Court of Wards appointed me to be your guardian. If I have at any time been unduly severe, I have no doubt the Lord Treasurer will take your part. But before you start shouting for vengeance, hadn't you better consider what case you have against me? I have not threatened to send you to Nunehead as a punishment for your flagrant misconduct, though plenty of people would maintain that you ought to be punished. Remembering that your lordship has now reached the advanced dignity of nineteen years, I hoped we could dispense with such forms of discipline. Was this the intention of a tyrant? I asked that you should make me certain promises, because I have a duty to restrain you from gambling away your fortune while you are still in my care. Do you think the Privy Council would view this matter exactly as you do? Do you think I should be censured for trying my hardest to preserve you from the folly of playing cards at Sutleigh? For that is the object of sending you to Nunehead: to keep you out of harm's way. I have offered you an honourable alternative. If you won't give me a promise of good behaviour, then that's your fault, not mine, and you mustn't blame me for shutting you up because you can't be trusted."

He paused, but John did not speak, being too much oppressed by the cunning logic of the arguments that were cutting the ground from under his feet.

"Perhaps I should warn you," continued the frigid voice, "that once you get to Nunehead you will have to stay there. You will be escorted by a suitable retinue of servants — my servants, by the way, not yours — under the direction of my chaplain. I need not remind you how many years Mr. Price has been a schoolmaster; he's not a man you can hope to cozen or intimidate. You can occupy yourself in writing to the Queen if you choose, but I don't advise it. If there's one thing she hates more than a rebel, it's a spendthrift. I don't think you'll get much help from that quarter."

There was an hour-glass in a carved frame on the table; Bernard drew it towards him.

206

"You need not go into exile," he said. "You have only to promise me that you will stick to the rules I have made for you. I'm still prepared to accept your word. But if you insist on defying me, I tell you this, John: I'll make you very sorry for it. You will be taken to Nunehead tomorrow, and everyone at Minton will hear the reason. The servants, our guests — Robert Evesham and the Howards, including Lucy — they will all know why you had to be banished from our summer pleasures here like a schoolboy in disgrace. Think of that before you make a final decision. You have five minutes to change your mind."

He up-ended the glass figure-of-eight, so that the sand began to trickle into the empty cone below. John watched him in a mood of furious despair. He had no doubt at all that Bernard would carry out his threats; there would be no escape from Nunehead, and nowhere he could go if he did escape — nowhere within reach of Tamsin, at any rate. And he couldn't take Tamsin away because he hadn't got any money, and he certainly wouldn't be able to get hold of any. Worst of all, it now transpired that Tamsin was bound to hear the whole story of his humiliation. This was intolerable.

He could prevent it of course, simply by making the necessary promises. After that he would no longer be able to enter her father's house, but at least he would remain at Minton and there were plenty of other places where they could meet. That would be a lot better than hopeless isolation at Nunehead.

An unbroken thread of sand was running through the neck of the hourglass. When the level reached the lowest notch on the frame, his five minutes would be over. He wished now that he hadn't chosen this particular occasion for challenging Bernard's authority. If it hadn't been for Tamsin, he would have felt inclined to go on fighting, put up with Nunehead and anything else his cousin could do to him, rather than surrender. But he couldn't face the double hardship of being separated from Tamsin, and of knowing how she must despise him for his futility and dependence. The rim of sand had risen to the five minute mark. Bernard looked up at him.

"Well? Which is it to be?"

"I — I'll do what you wish, sir. If I can stay at Minton."

The low murmur was almost inaudible, and he felt sick with mortification. He half expected Bernard to crow over him now he had won such a complete victory. But Bernard took his triumph very quietly. He made John recite his promise in a definite form (there was no wriggling out of that) and said no more about it.

He sent for Edmund Royden and for Giles, and got down to the tedious business of discovering when and where the various pieces of plate had been sold, so that Royden could go to Garth and try to buy them back. No precious fragment of the Harcourt possessions must be allowed to melt away during the Baron's minority.

By the time all this was over, it was far too late for John to meet Tamsin on the hill above Sutleigh. The poor girl must have gone home hours ago. And he was faced with the disagreeable fact that he could no longer spend the night with her in her father's house. This evening he dared not even take the risk of sending a message. Giles was already in deep enough water because he had sold the missing plate. There was the young groom Jenkyn; he could have been trusted to carry a letter to Tamsin in the ordinary way, but John had a shrewd idea that all his servants were being badgered and bullied by Finch, who knew that something had been going on behind his back but couldn't make out what it was. It would be very unwise to send Jenkyn off on a secret errand tonight, and there was no one else. John's heart contracted painfully when he thought of Tamsin lying there in that room he had come to know so well, and wondering what had gone wrong. It did not make things any easier when he reflected how intensely he was going to dislike telling her.

★ ★ ★

Tamsin had spent a disappointing afternoon at the lair in the bracken, as the happy glow of anticipation slowly died away, and she got cold and cramped. At last she had gone home, buoying herself up with the certainty that John would come this evening instead.

She went to bed early, and actually fell asleep, to wake three hours later with a guilty jump, half dreaming that she had heard his footsteps in the garden below. She slipped on her wedding ring, and lay in bed listening for him.

But he did not come.

She could not understand it. She could guess how some trivial event might have held him up this afternoon, but in that case he would either have made a point of coming this evening, or else he would have sent Giles over with a letter.

Suppose he was ill? Too ill to write. She kept telling herself that this was nonsense, and that Giles would have let her know. But would he? He would not want to distress her, and he certainly wouldn't want her in tears at the patient's bedside, unless he was so desperately ill that the secret of their marriage no longer mattered. She could not rely on Giles to tell her anything until it was too late. There was a rumour of small pox in a village just beyond Gaultonsbury . . .

By the next morning she knew there was nothing for it: she would have to go to Minton Gabriel and spy out the land. She nibbled a distracted breakfast, put on her most elegant habit, and set out on Grey Vanity.

She could not enquire for John, so she had decided to pay a call on Charity Rivers, who had continued as one of Lady Kettering's waiting-gentlewomen after her marriage. Tamsin had never visited her before, but she knew that Honor Mulcaster often went to see her sister. In the course of a short gossip she would soon find out if anything extraordinary had happened to John.

It seemed a sensible scheme with no pitfalls, but as she approached the house she found herself growing steadily more nervous and over-awed. She had not realised quite how small she would feel, riding into the forecourt alone under the stare of the sixty-five windows. Perhaps she should have brought a groom? She dismounted, knocked on the big, iron-studded door, and by this time she knew she ought to have brought a groom, because what on earth was she to do with her horse? She stood there holding on to his reins and feeling a fool.

The door was opened by a retainer wearing the Kettering livery who treated her with the secure disdain of a man who knew that his employers looked down on her.

"Mrs. Rivers?" repeated the retainer, as though he had never heard the name before.

"I should like to see her. If you please," added Tamsin, smouldering slightly. She wondered if he was going to send her round to the back door.

"Mrs. Rivers will be attending on her ladyship at this hour. Besides which, the house is full of guests; I doubt if it will be convenient," said the disdainful one. He then padded away, leaving Tamsin in a state of uncertainty on the doorstep, though to give him his due, he could hardly invite her to bring Grey Vanity into the hall.

Tamsin peeped inside and breathed the rarefied air of Minton Gabriel, where all the rooms were light and high, and every item of costly furniture was endlessly polished and furbished and cared for by hordes of exemplary servants. A troop of children ran across the hall and up the stairs: Walter and James and Eliza Kettering with several of their cousins, pushing and laughing. And Henry Lethbridge, the gentleman-usher, was talking to one of the household musicians. There must be the usual consort of strings during supper, and they would probably want to dance in the gallery later.

Whatever had happened to John, he certainly was not dead or dying.

The retainer padded back again, followed by Charity, hurrying and rather put out.

"Tamsin! What's the matter? Why have you come?"

This was not very encouraging.

"Just to pay you a visit."

"You've never been before."

"No. But your mother and Honor often do. Is there any harm in my coming?"

"No harm at all, I am delighted to see you," said Charity, who quite plainly was not. "It's just that this is not a very good time, when her ladyship has so many guests. The work of the house is doubled, and besides — "

The words trailed off, but Tamsin caught the drift of what Charity had stopped herself from saying: the Ketterings are the kindest and friendliest of country neighbours, but after all they do belong to a different world, and it's not for the rest of us to edge our way in, when part of that world overlaps into Minton Gabriel.

And where the Mulcasters would not come uninvited. Tamsin could imagine how her own incursion would appear: that wanton from Sutleigh, inventing a lame excuse and hanging round the place, avid for men. She had been so preoccupied that none of this had dawned on her before, but now her one desire was to get away as quickly as possible, without waiting for news of John, for it was obvious that no great disaster had overtaken him, and she had been a fool to get into a panic.

She was beginning to withdraw, and Charity was feebly protesting, when a party of ladies and gentlemen emerged from a room at the back of the hall and bore down on the open doorway: Sir Bernard and Lady Kettering, with Mr.

Howard and Lady Dorothy, Sir Robert Evesham, Sir Bernard's brother Richard and various other guests. Tamsin had no time to fade out of sight; they all came filing out, and there was nothing else she could do but stand there, still holding on to Vanity who had just staled on the clean gravel.

Sir Bernard gave her a very civil greeting, his wife acknowledged her curtsey rather more stiffly and then they both waited, sure that there must be some extraordinary reason for Tamsin to arrive on their doorstep. It was a dreadful moment.

She was rescued by Evesham, who recognised her with enthusiasm.

"Mrs. Grove, I am delighted to see you again. I have been intending to ride over and visit your father, but I was not sure whether this would be convenient to him, and I wanted to consult you first."

"That is very kind of you, Sir Robert," said Tamsin. In fact, her father disliked meeting the friends of his youth and did his best to avoid them, and she was grateful for Evesham's tact. He noticed her hesitation and changed the subject, reminding her of their first meeting.

"If you hadn't been there, I dare say we should still be wandering among the moors and mountains — unless we had circumnavigated the globe and come upon Minton from the opposite direction!"

Alexander Howard joined in the conversation. By now everyone was standing round them, and Ann Kettering felt obliged to say that Mrs Grove might care to join them on their walk to the lake.

Tamsin found that some minion was removing Vanity from her grasp, and then that she was strolling beside Evesham through the formal gardens where everything seemed slightly artificial and intangible, as in a dream. Paths of crushed shells led past blazing beds of snapdragons and marigolds, laid out in a fantastic design of wheels and whorls and flourishes; hollyhocks and sun-flowers grew tall in front of prettily coloured trellises. They came to a paved arena containing some rare shrubs and a bestiary of wooden birds and animals. They were painted an icy white which looked quite startling against the darkness of a yew hedge.

She pulled herself out of her daze and said at random that she supposed Sir Robert knew the names of all the plants. "For you have made a study of botany, have you not?"

"What makes you think so?"

"Why, from the description of exotic flowers and trees in your *Account of a Journey into Bohemia.*"

"Do you mean to say you have read that?" Evesham was delighted, much more so than she would have expected. She had never met an author before. "Alexander — Mrs. Grove has read my book!"

Howard pretended to find this incredible, and invented various unflattering ways in which she might have come across Evesham's masterpiece.

"You had it from a huckster at a fair, Mrs. Grove: is it not so? Given away free with a penn'orth of pins, but you won't admit it in case Sir Robert should take offence."

Tamsin laughed and shook her head, not at all wanting to say how she had got hold of the book, because she had borrowed it from John. She was relieved when someone changed the subject by asking Evesham when he meant to go abroad again.

"In the spring, I hope."

"Is it true," asked Richard Kettering, "that you mean to take John Harcourt with you?"

"If I can get permission from Her Majesty. And from your brother."

Sir Bernard was just ahead of them. He said drily that anyone who took Harcourt abroad would have his hands full.

Tamsin, candidly eavesdropping, absorbed the startling fact that John might be going abroad. Did he know? Did he want to go?

They were approaching the lake, an oblong stretch of water which Sir Bernard had constructed by diverting a couple of small streams and letting them flow into a disused cattle-pond. By now Tamsin had gathered that one of the girls staying in the house had challenged two others to an angling match, and the whole party had turned out to see the result, for the time allowed was nearly over.

There was such a lot of noise and hilarity on the bank that every carp, dace and gudgeon in the lake had gone down to the muddy bottom and stayed there, but the three contestants did not seem to mind. One of them had got her line entangled in the reeds, and her two friends were shrieking advice. Each of the girls had a swain in attendance to bait their hooks. Tamsin's gaze passed indifferently over two of the couples. Between them, Lucy Howard was hopefully holding her rod over the water as if it was a magician's wand. John was sitting in the grass at her feet.

"What, has none of you had a nibble?" asked Sir Bernard, surveying the empty baskets.

Peals of merriment, as one of the girls announced: "Lucy caught a pickled herring."

"I am ashamed of you, Lucy," said her father. "You might have chosen a fresh-water fish to cheat with."

"You should lay the blame on Lord Harcourt. He fixed it to my hook when I wasn't attending."

"What an ungrateful girl you are,"

complained John. "I was making sure that you won. We simply need to say that my cousin has filled the lake with vinegar and keeps it stocked with spiced fish swimming about ready for the table."

"Excellent," said Sir Bernard, laughing. "Surely you know, my dear Howard, that a vinegar-lake is the latest notion in husbandry?"

John was getting up when he caught sight of Tamsin. For a brief instant his expression was completely revealing, and she would not have been surprised if he had stepped backwards into the lake. Then the vizor came down, the practised mask of cool courtesy behind which he had learnt to hide from a continual public scrutiny. He did not speak to her, it was impossible to single her out in such a crowd. They remained about three yards apart and quite unable to communicate.

Then Robert Evesham took her arm and they moved away.

The main party was wending its way back, and as soon as they reached the house Tamsin asked for her horse and said she must go home. Vanity was restored to her and she rode off alone down the avenue.

She took the return journey very slowly, being in no hurry to get back to shabby, neglected Sutleigh, or to Margery's probing curiosity. She felt too forlorn already.

Naturally she did not suspect John of deceiving her with Lucy Howard; she recognised that there was bound to be a certain amount of harmless gallantry among the young men and girls who were now staying at Minton. But she could not help wishing he had not seemed quite so happy this morning, after he had failed to keep their assignation and had left her in suspense; he must know how wretched she would be feeling.

She was following a track through the woods, and had just reached the top of the hill between the two combes, when she heard the sound of hoofbeats, and looking round, caught a splash of something alien between the trees — the kingfisher blue of John's doublet, and the gleaming chestnut shoulder of the Barb. Her spirits reviving, she stopped and waited for them to join her.

Forgetting discretion for once, John had followed her as soon and as fast as he could manage. It was a hot morning and he was out of breath; his opening was a little unfortunate.

"What possessed you to come to Minton? You know how careful we have to be."

"Good grief, I thought you were on your deathbed! How do you suppose I felt, when you never came near me all yesterday, never sent a message — what were you doing, anyway? Being careful — or disporting yourself with Lucy Howard?"

"I'm sorry. I was going to ride over after dinner and explain." He sat loosely in the saddle, fanning himself with his hat, while he collected his wits and his manners. "Forgive me, sweetheart. I would have given anything to come to you last night, but I couldn't help it, truly. My cousin has found out about the money I lost playing hazard with Toby Strange, and I got an interminable homily — "

"But that was long ago, in April, and it wasn't such a vast sum either.

223

How did Sir Bernard find out? I don't understand."

"I can't go into it now," said John hurriedly. "And the amount doesn't signify, because they are all so afraid I might take after some of my prodigal forbears that there would be an outcry if I lost a groat at post and pair with the children. Which shows how foolish our revered elders can be, for I wouldn't care if I never played again. The worst of it is that I've had to promise not to pay any more visits to your father's house, and that is the most infernal hindrance."

"Well, you don't often visit my father."

"My dear heart, I visit him nearly every night, even if he doesn't know it. Now I shall no longer be able to come to the Manor; we shall have to devise some other way of meeting."

"Oh. Surely your agreement can't include that? You never gamble at Sutleigh now."

"Granted. What would you like me to tell my cousin? 'I simply go there to lie with my wife'?"

"Why tell him anything at all? He'll never know whether you come or not."

John said, rather austerely, "I have made a promise, and I cannot break it."

"You made me a promise also. In church, do you remember?" She saw John's stricken expression, and said quickly, "I don't mean to be unkind, love. Only I cannot for the life of me see why you were unwise enough to commit yourself. You're not a child that he can tell you what houses you may or may not enter."

This was exactly where John's double-dealing was bound to land him in trouble. He had given Tamsin a totally wrong impression of his relationship with Bernard, and he had hidden from Bernard the relationship with Tamsin as though it had never existed, and the result was that everything he did was incomprehensible to one or other of them.

He tried to get himself out of the present impasse by saying that he hadn't cared to be obstructive in case Bernard began to look more closely into his reasons for visiting Sutleigh. Tamsin still seemed dissatisfied, and he was goaded to attack as a substitute for a weak defence.

"If only your father and his friends hadn't made Sutleigh so notorious — '

"Are you blaming me for that?"

"I'm not blaming you for anything, sweetheart, but it's a pity that we should have to suffer as a consequence."

"You don't appear to be suffering unduly."

"Do you suggest I was enjoying that mummery this morning?"

"You'll always enjoy any woman you can get hold of," retorted Tamsin, whose afflictions had made her feel coarse and unreasonable.

John lost his temper. "My God, I'll make you unsay that!"

"You have leave to try — if you can demean yourself so far as to enter a house that belongs to your father-in-law."

She tugged at Vanity's reins, gave him a sharp prod with her heel, and started down the hill towards Sutleigh.

After a few moments she heard a commotion of cracking twigs and crashing branches behind her, and knew that he had decided to give chase. Vanity pricked up his ears. Tamsin's response was instinctive: she kicked him on, and he broke into a canter.

This was the second time she had run away from John. Today he was on horseback too, and on a much faster horse. He was gaining ground. It was broad enough here for him to come abreast of her and get hold of her reins; a little further on the track narrowed, above the precipice of an old quarry — if she got as far as that, he would not be able to pass. She urged Vanity on; as they reached the narrowest strip the Barb came thundering downhill after them, and she realised with horror that John was going to overtake her on the quarry side. It was mad, impossible, the Barb must be completely out of control. Tamsin steered Vanity as far in to the right as she could. Glancing down to the left, she was appalled to see how little ground there was to spare before the edge dropped thirty feet sheer to the bed of the quarry. The Barb was hurling into that small space, John's saddle bumped her knee, she heard herself scream. Horse and rider seemed to be poised over the empty air. And then, miraculously, they were ahead of her, and John, far from losing control, was bringing the mare round in one of those superb half-turns so that they were right across the way, and Vanity was forced to a shuddering standstill.

John dismounted and went to his head. Tamsin looked at the hoofmarks on the crumbling rim of the path, and felt sick.

"You might have been killed," she whispered.

He was not interested in this speculation. He said: "Get down."

She got down. He led the horses into a clearing a short way ahead where he let them graze, they were too blown to wander off. She eyed him apprehensively. There was something daunting about that sulky and imperious profile. He came back to her, caught her roughly by the shoulders.

"So you accuse me of dallying with other women. I've wronged you, it seems. What evidence can you bring against me? Let us have chapter and verse."

"But I didn't intend to accuse you," she protested. "It was a jest, merely."

"A sufficiently wry one." He stared

down at her. "Doesn't it strike you that you are the last person who should pay attention to imaginary scandals? Don't you know what kind of stories I have overheard about you and the men who surround you? I don't believe a word of them, and that goes without saying. I would trust you anywhere. And I think you might have the grace to trust me, at least at Minton among my cousin's guests."

"Oh," said Tamsin, flushing. She could guess only too accurately the sort of rumours that he must have heard about her, and how bitter it must be for him to be obliged to listen in silence without defending her. He had some excuse for complaining that her home was notorious. It was kinder than saying that she was notorious — and that she had made a spectacle of herself by rushing over to Minton, uninvited.

"I'm sorry, John. I do trust you, and I swear to you I didn't come to spy on you because I was jealous. I admit I did feel a few pangs when I got there — but only from seeing you all so merry together."

John's heart was melted. "My poor

darling, what a brute I am to reproach you. When you ought to have been by my side, when you're the one girl I want, and we treat you like a stranger. And it's no fault of yours, which makes it ten times more cruel."

They clung to each other, kissing and patching up their first quarrel. Tamsin made no more attempts to talk him into breaking his promise and coming to Sutleigh, and it was she who suggested presently that they must find another meeting-place.

"What's that building about fifty yards along from your gate?" asked John. "Is it a granary of some sort? If we could use that, you would not have far to go, and there are no other houses nearby."

"The tithe-barn?" she said doubtfully. "Hardly the lodging I should choose. However, I dare say it would do. Until next month, at least, when they start getting the harvest in."

"We'll have found something better by then," said John with a careless optimism.

They arranged to go to the tithe-barn that evening. John had managed to skate round the true cause of his difficulties better than he had expected, and he hoped that Tamsin would now accept the new restrictions without asking any further questions.

★ ★ ★

John and Tamsin told each other that meeting at the tithe-barn was like living in a pastoral, or in the fairy-tale atmosphere of their wedding night at the hunting-lodge. This was not true, but it served them for the first week.

Unfortunately it had rained on the feast of St. Swithin, and there was every sign that the usual forty days would follow. The tithe-barn leaked, because the Lord of the Manor was too lazy to have the roof mended, and for the first time John told Tamsin what he thought of the ruinous way her father neglected his property. Tamsin retorted with spirit. There was nothing wrong with the roof of the manor house, and they would be snug enough under that if John hadn't made a lot of silly and unnecessary promises, regardless of any promise he might have made to her. This led to a rather childish quarrel, after which they kissed and made friends and made love again, so that all seemed to be well.

But the same thing happened every time they met. The later disagreements were generally begun by Tamsin, for John was trying hard not to provoke her. It was not what he said that annoyed her, so much as what he did, or more often didn't, couldn't or wouldn't do. John was so much occupied with his cousin's guests, he had so many engagements; she was always free whenever he wanted her, he was the one who had to say he couldn't come tomorrow or the next day, he'd do his best, but he couldn't be sure . . . Tamsin found this humiliating.

Also she was now undeniably jealous, not of what he might be doing with any particular girl, but of all the women at Minton who had the privilege of dancing or riding with him, singing or playing billiards, strolling with him in the long gallery, engaged in the deep discussions and allusive jokes that grew up among any group of people spending several weeks together in the same house. Being excluded from all this hurt so much that Tamsin couldn't help sharpening her claws on him occasionally, and somehow that turned into a habit of nagging. This horrified her, but she didn't seem able to stop.

I'll be different tonight, she told herself, on the last evening in July, waiting for him in the darkness of the barn. They could not have a light, in case it was seen from the lane. The tithe-barn was practically empty, except for a loose pile of hay, about eight foot square, in one corner. It smelt musty, because of the damp, but it made a bed for them, so they could not afford to grumble. Although it was so empty, the barn creaked and rustled unceasingly, and she hated being there alone. She didn't mind the scurrying rats and mice, there were plenty of those at the manor, but she was sure there were bats as well. If only John would come.

I won't scold him, she thought, however late he is. I won't be a vixen.

So that when at last he arrived, she was ostentatiously quiet and well-bred. John was quiet too, perhaps he had been making the same resolutions. Hand in hand, they found their way over to the heaped hay and sat down, still on the defensive.

"At least, it's not raining."

"No. But I think it soon will be."

As though we were strangers, she thought. This was almost worse than squabbling.

"There's much more water in the stream — "

"Evesham was telling me this morning—"

They both stopped.

"Go on," she said. "What about Evesham?"

"This morning, when it was too wet to ride, he got all his maps out, and showed me the journey he wants to make next spring. I think he does mean to take me, Tamsin. Provided I can get a passport; that means permission from Her Majesty, but I can't think why she should refuse."

"Oh."

The cold little monosyllable checked him.

"You don't mind, do you, love? You don't expect me to spend all my days in England?"

234

"No, of course I don't."

She took it for granted that he would want to travel abroad. He would want to fight in the wars. If the Earl of Essex led another expedition to help the Protestants in France, John would be spoiling to go. She did not welcome the idea, but it was one that any woman these days must be prepared for, and she felt she could accept it quite calmly once she was acknowledged and established as John's wife; it was her present rootless condition that made her dislike the thought of his going too far away.

When she said this, John did not agree.

"I'd much rather go while I've got to be away from you anyway. It will help to make the two years pass quicker."

"But it won't be two years!" she said, aghast.

"I shan't be abroad more than a few months. I was thinking of the time we've got to wait before I come of age. Since we'll have to live apart, I might just as well be in Italy as in England."

He felt her stiffen beside him, and received a curious sense of opposition, as though a hedgehog had put out all its prickles. "Tamsin, what's the matter? You've known all along that we shall have to face these separations. Two months from now, at the beginning of October, my cousin will take his family to London for the winter. They go up every year, you know that. You can't have thought that I should be staying behind?"

"Oh no. But I hope by then I may be pregnant."

"You *hope* you may be pregnant?" repeated John, thunderstruck.

"Yes," she said simply. "I pray every night for a son. Not just because I want to bear your child, though I do long for that too, but chiefly so that we can put an end to this secrecy. I know I can't endure it much longer. If I was breeding, we could go to your cousin and tell him the truth, and our troubles would soon be over."

"What makes you think so?" he enquired.

"Why, you told me so yourself, the day you asked me to marry you."

"Tamsin, you must have misunderstood me, I can't have said any such thing."

236

"Yes, you did. You said that Sir Bernard might seek to get our marriage annulled, but that once we had a child on the way we should be safe, because he would never do anything to endanger the rights of your heir."

There was a short pause.

"Well," she challenged him. "You're not going to deny it?"

"I may have said that if you had a child, they would be obliged to recognise our marriage without delay. I'd still prefer not to have the news come out until I am twenty-one and my own master."

"But why, John? Why?" She was incredulous. "You must want to get it over and done with so that we can be together."

"Yes, my dear life, but it won't be all plain sailing, and I don't relish quarrelling with my cousin — "

"I take it you'd sooner quarrel with me?"

"Will you listen and not interrupt? I don't want to fall out with Bernard while he still has control of my money. It will be difficult to set up our own household — "

"Oh, what does that signify?" She brushed aside his excuses. "There is only one way Sir Bernard can hurt us, and you say he won't try to do that if I have a child, so what else is there to make a song about? I dare say there will be some lesser evils to put up with, and some hard words exchanged, but you must have learnt to stand up to your guardian by now. Anyone would think you were afraid of him."

John did not answer.

Tamsin hadn't the faintest suspicion that she might have hit the nail on the head; that remark was merely meant to sting him out of his inertia. It would not have occurred to her that he was afraid of anybody. He was a superbly tough and masculine young man, physically fearless, a dominating lover, and that impressive degree older and more experienced than she was herself, with a graceful maturity of manner that was the product of his birth and upbringing. She knew he was attached to Sir Bernard, and they always seemed to her to be on very good terms.

She went on searching in her mind for

a key to his reluctance, oblivious of the fact that she had already found one.

"I don't believe you want anyone to know that I'm your wife. I suppose you're ashamed of me."

"For pity's sake, Tamsin — "

"You were ashamed of me the day I came to Minton. You were far better employed hanging around that little milk-faced Lucy."

"You are talking absolute nonsense!"

Tamsin half realised this, but her voice had run away with her, the whine rising to a pitch that was dangerously close to hysteria.

"It's all changed, I don't count any more. At the outset nothing was too good for me, but now I have to come down here to this stinking hole and wait till it pleases your lordship to arrive, and you're always late nowadays. I've waited hours and hours here alone, and I know there are bats!"

"My darling girl, you are mistaken in every particular — except perhaps the bats, and I hope you may be wrong about them too."

John was using his soft, bantering tone,

which this evening failed to charm her. He slid a competent arm under her shoulders in the darkness, while his other hand ran possessively down her body from the breast to the thigh.

"Let me go!" she almost screamed, giving him a vicious jab in the ribs with her elbow as she rolled away from him in the hay. "I won't be pawed about to suit your convenience. That's all you ever want me for, isn't it? All you come here for?"

"It seems I can do nothing right," he said acidly. "First I neglect you, and then I am too demanding. And if there is a grain of truth in your second accusation, is that so great a crime for a man who is not yet two months married? Come, sweetheart, you have never refused to let me love you before."

"I don't feel as though we are married," sobbed Tamsin.

"What the devil do you mean by that?"

She was lying with her face pressed into the thin scratchy hay, and the dust choked her. She raised her head a little, coughing and crying.

"Married people live in the same house — lie together in a proper bed. You drag me to this filthy barn — and I feel as though — as though I was a kitchenmaid creeping out to fornicate with the stable-boy."

After this there was a silence so arctic that Tamsin stopped crying, knowing that she had gone too far. John was standing up now, she had felt the weight shift from his side of the hay. She could not see him; it was part of the nightmare that the barn was pitch black on a moonless night, and they had not seen each other since they came in.

"What are you doing?" she asked.

"Going home. There seems no purpose in my staying here."

Whatever she had wanted from him, it was not that.

She began to nag at him again. "I dare say you don't care to be compared with a stable-boy?"

John left her without another word.

August

BY the next morning Tamsin was feeling ashamed of her outburst, and wondering how soon she could meet John and put things right between them. They had parted last night without making any plans, but the weather had cleared into a calm, golden day with a feeling about it that everything was meant to go well, and her hopes soared when she looked out of the staircase window and saw Jenkyn riding through the gate on one of John's horses.

He could not come to Sutleigh himself, but apparently he could send his groom; how ridiculous men were over matters of honour.

There was a letter for her. She took it to her bedchamber and read what he had to say.

Madam,
Considering the reproaches you made

me last night, and the distress such encounters must cause you, I think it better we do not meet again until I can provide a setting more worthy of you, where you may enjoy the soft living and proper attentions that seem necessary before you are able to take any pleasure in my company. I am sorry that I have lately inveigled you into such a wretched place. I did not suppose that your affection would prove to be so dependent on circumstance.

I rest your ladyship's assured servant at commandment,
John Harcourt de Laleham

She had to read this through twice before it made sense, and then she could hardly believe it. He did not wish to see her. He was trying to punish her for losing her temper (while remaining quite indifferent to his own failings, which he ignored). All of which was bad enough, but the diabolical part was the way he had twisted her objections to the tithe-barn, so that she was made to appear as a blatant mercenary who had married him entirely for his worldly advantages. He could not have written her a more unpleasant letter if he had sat up all night composing it. Perhaps he had.

There was no possible reply to such an insult. She went down to make it plain to Jenkyn who was refreshing himself in the kitchen; he must be sure to tell his lordship that she had read his letter and there was no answer.

Then she locked herself in her room and cried for two hours.

During the next few days she existed in a kind of limbo, hearing and seeing nothing of John, thinking of nothing else. Her feelings altered constantly as she was driven this way and that by her emotions, as wild as a weathercock.

Sometimes she had a fit of remorse because she had said such cruel things to him at the tithe-barn, and unless she admitted this she could hardly blame him for staying away. In contrast she would remember how specious and selfish he was being — why should she go crawling to that arrogant monster who had never once put himself out for her? As for saying that he was her assured servant at commandment, it was a piece of damned impudence, and she would like to tell him so.

She was beginning to get a ridiculous sense of panic as she realised how totally she was cut off from him.

There was only one person who moved freely between Sutleigh and Minton, and that was her half-brother. Ever since he had defended old Salathiel the ballad-singer from the boys who were tormenting him in the stocks, both John and Sir Bernard had taken an interest in Simon. They must know very well that his own home was a bad place for him to hang around in idleness, and he had a standing invitation to Minton now that his summer holiday had begun, to take part in any sport that happened to be going, or help exercise the horses.

She watched him enviously as he set out early one morning, wondering whether he could be pressed into service as a messenger. At fourteen he was still curiously blind to certain aspects of life — probably to protect himself from noticing some of the things that went on at Sutleigh. She thought he was too young to be burdened with the secret of her marriage. At least he would be able to give her some news of John when he came home.

He arrived back full of information, and she did not have to dig for it, everything came bubbling out.

"His lordship let me take his Barbary mare out to the paddock for a gallop, which was a high favour, for in general he won't allow anyone else to handle her except Jenkyn. She is a beautiful creature, and so gentle; she follows his lordship around like a dog. His lordship is pacing a young horse for Sir Bernard, teaching him to amble. Sir Bernard says he has the best hands of anyone he ever knew, and he can break in colts as well as an Italian riding-master. I heard him saying so to Mr. Howard . . . Oh, and I am going to hunt on Wednesday; his lordship says he will mount me. The assembly is at the hunting-lodge, and there is a great old hart up there in the wilderness that they have been after for years — "

"At the hunting-lodge?" repeated Tamsin, with a choking sensation in her throat. "Are you — do they propose to sleep there overnight?"

"No, there are too many ladies and gentlemen going from the great house, there wouldn't be enough space. We are to start very early and meet at the lodge for a hunt breakfast. You can come too, if you care to," added Simon as an afterthought.

"I should not dream of pushing my way in uninvited."

"But you were invited. That's what I'm telling you."

"Was I?" she asked eagerly. "By whom?"

"By Sir Bernard, I suppose. He is the host. Or was it his lordship? It was he who asked if I would like to go, and someone said I must bring my sister — but I think that may have been later, after his lordship had gone away. So it must have been Sir Bernard who spoke of my sister. Unless it was Sir Robert or Mr. Howard."

He could not be more definite than that, and Tamsin was in a quandary. If John had invited her, or manœuvred someone else into suggesting her name, then it was an olive-branch; she could go to the hunting-lodge knowing that they were reconciled.

On the other hand it was just as likely that she had been included because Sir Bernard thought it uncivil to ask Simon and leave her out. The neighbourly offer of a day's hunting was not the same as an invitation to Minton Gabriel.

And if John didn't want her to join the party, it would be unbearable, especially at the hunting-lodge, where they had first been together in that state of exquisite happiness. What on earth was she to do?

In the end she decided that she would have to risk a letter enclosing it in one to Giles Brown. Surely that would be unostentatious and reasonably safe?

She spent the whole evening on it.

My very good lord,

I hear from my brother that we are bidden to hunt with you on Wednesday, but I can by no means discover who it was that wished for me to accompany Simon, whether it was your lordship or Sir Bernard. Will

248

it please you to tell me what I am to do? If you desire it, I shall come to the assembly most joyfully, but if not, I would far rather stay at home than incur your displeasure. My dear lord, I hope you will send for me to come. It is now six days since I received any word from you. I am sure that you do not believe all those hard things you wrote of me in your letter. If I have offended you, I beg your pardon, and ask you to remember that all my words and actions have been governed by a love that is impatient to be free of hindrances. Dear heart, be kind to me. I pray God will have you always in His keeping, and rest your lordship's most loving and obedient wife.

Tamsin Harcourt de Laleham

This was her fourth effort, and when she read it through she nearly tore it up, like all the others, because it was too servile. But it did represent a very fair summary of her feelings, and after all, John's obedient wife was what she had promised to be; in those encounters at the tithe-barn she had fallen a long way short of her promises, and perhaps it was good for her to humble herself a little.

She intended to send Simon to Minton in the morning, and it was tiresome to find that he had gone off to Gaultonsbury to visit a friend from the Grammar School. She sent her father's groom instead; he delivered the letter to one of the liveried retainers, who assured him that Mr. Brown would receive it directly he came in to dinner.

So immediately after her own dinner, Tamsin established herself in the staircase window, with a strategic view of the gateway and a short stretch of the lane. She watched from two till seven, and not a soul came through the gate.

She had missed her supper; she still lingered by the window until it was too dark to see, and only then recognised the fact that he was not going to answer.

There was naturally no question of her hunting now. Simon set off before dawn. She did not get up to see him start, but all through that silent and lonely day she thought of the gay cavalcade and pictured them streaming across the hills to the brave music of the horn.

During the afternoon she set herself to weeding the herb garden, a thankless task, but it gave herself something to do.

The sun was beating on her neck as she plucked up straggles of ground elder from among the scented leaves of mint and balm. Behind her in the kitchen court one of the maids was singing as she hung up the washing.

"Oh, love is handsome and love is
    fine
And love's a jewel while it is new,
But when 'tis old it waxeth cold
And fades away like the morning
    dew . . . "

It was hot in the garden, but Tamsin shivered. "I don't understand what's happening to us," she whispered. "I don't understand."

She was still standing hopelessly in the middle of the unkempt herb garden, when Margery called from the house, "Do stop mooning and come indoors. I've a surprise for you."

The only surprise Tamsin wanted could

not possibly happen today, when she knew John was up at the hunting-lodge. However, she went back into the house, and as she blinked in the gloom of the shadowy hall, a pair of arms came out and caught her.

"Well, my queen of hearts, how have you been conducting yourself without me?" demanded Toby Strange.

"Oh, Toby! How glad I am to see you again."

And this was true. A moment earlier she had felt she could care for no one who wasn't John, but Toby was such a very old and dear friend, and so entertaining, and it was over three months since he had gone away.

He was worn and dusty from travelling, glad to kick off his boots and sit down in the cool stone hall, while the two young women brought him wine and fruit, and asked about his adventures in London.

He'd had a fairly prosperous summer, he told them. Of course there were always disappointments, but there did seem to be an uncommonly large number of people who wanted to get rid of their money; they made new acquaintances so confidingly, played cards so frequently — and so badly.

"This sad addiction to gaming will be the ruin of our nation," said Toby, shaking his head portentously.

Tamsin had never approved of the way Toby made a living, battening on the very young or ignorant who could not resist his wiles. She remembered how hard he had tried to fleece John.

"You ought to be ashamed of yourself."

"Yes, I ought," he agreed with enthusiasm. "Do you think you could reform me? And as a first step, do you think you could give me a bed for the night? I meant to lodge at the White Swan, but a company of players has just arrived there, and they are in a turmoil."

Of course he must stay as long as he wished. A curious alliance had grown up over the years between Toby and the Groves, with the result that Sutleigh was the nearest thing he had to a home.

Tamsin went off to prepare a bedchamber for him. Toby put down his goblet, frowning.

"What's amiss with her?" he asked Margery.

"You can tell there's something wrong?"

"She's like a little ghost, and all the sparkle's gone. What's happened?"

"I'm afraid she must have quarrelled with Lord Harcourt. He's fairly bewitched her — "

"Harcourt?"

"Yes, she became his mistress some time in May, soon after you left, and for a while they were dotingly in love with each other. She's never said a word to me, mark you; young madam has always had her nose in the air — not that I bear any grudge; I was glad to see her so happy. But he's given up visiting her now, and just lately she's taken to shutting herself in her chamber and weeping. I hope it's not a case for the midwife."

"I'm sure it's nothing of the kind," retorted Toby. "No young sprig of a lordling is likely to put Tamsin in danger of the midwife."

Everything Margery said on this subject was liable to be exaggerated and distorted; she had credited Tamsin with about eight imaginary lovers in the last year. And Tamsin did not take lovers, as Toby had

254

the best of reasons for knowing. He had been patiently trying to change her mind ever since she was fifteen.

All the same there was something the matter with her; he could not find out any more at present, for Margery was in a state of high dudgeon, and he had scarcely soothed her down when Tom Grove and old Gregory Timberlake appeared from different corners of the house where they had each been sleeping away the dullness of the afternoon in preparation for the evening's drinking. They were delighted to see Toby, and decided to open a fresh cask of canary in his honour.

They were gathered round the supper table when Simon came home; dirty, exhausted and exuberant.

"We had a splendid hunt," he announced. "I never rode so hard in my life, and I'm starving hungry — but it was fine sport; I wish you'd been there, Tamsin. You were a fool not to come."

Tamsin took no notice of this. "Have you gone blind or lost your manners?" she enquired in a rather waspish, elder sisterly way. "Aren't you going to greet Mr. Strange?"

"Oh, good evening, sir, have you come from London?" asked Simon with a complete absence of curiosity. He did not wait for an answer, "I was saying, we had excellent sport — "

"I wish you would at least wash your hands before you sit down to eat with us."

"Let him alone, girl," said their father indulgently.

In a dim recess of his mind where Tom Grove had occasional twinges of concern about his children, he had felt some satisfaction recently because Simon was being accepted by men like Kettering and young Harcourt, whose patronage might one day be invaluable. He wanted to hear how the boy had got on.

Simon was only too ready to tell him. "The woodmen had harboured a great stag for us; they were up there all yesterday, tracking him to his lair, and slept last night at the lodge; his lordship went with them. He is marvellously skilled in woodcraft and venery. They harboured this hart royal, and he broke covert and ran down wind towards Pargrave. We hunted him for an hour, and then the cunning old brute doubled back and ran through the whole herd, so that hounds lost him and picked up a new scent — you can imagine how Sir Bernard was fuming at his huntsman. Still, it was a warrantable beast, and we had relays of fresh hounds to hunt him with, so we went round full circle and killed at Wilfred's Tower. He was a hart of ten, and he gave us a good run for our trouble."

Simon helped himself to a leg of cold capon and took a huge bite out of it. He went on discoursing, between mouthfuls, on the prowess and horsemanship of everyone who had been at the hunt. There was a great deal about his lordship.

"Were there many ladies out?" asked Tamsin.

"A good number. Lady Kettering didn't go very far, but that Lady Dorothy, she's a tigress. I never heard a woman swear so. And her daughter Lucy, you might not think it, but she is a surpassing rider. Just as well if she's going to marry his lordship; otherwise she'd never see him."

"Going to marry Lord Harcourt?" squawked Margery, with one eye on Tamsin.

"Yes, didn't I tell you? The Minton people were all talking of it. They say the betrothal will be announced as soon as Sir Bernard and Mr. Howard have finished haggling over the settlements."

"It's not possible," breathed Tamsin.

Margery gave Toby a smart kick on the ankle, as though to say, I told you so. She then very good-naturedly covered up Tamsin's obvious confusion by listening to everything Simon predicted about the betrothal celebrations, and wondering whether they would roast a whole ox.

Toby managed to change the subject; he told Simon about the players who had arrived in Gaultonsbury and would be performing in the courtyard of the White Swan tomorrow afternoon.

"Would you like to go and see them?"

"Yes, indeed I would," said Simon.

He had at last finished his supper. Thankfully Toby pushed back his stool from the table.

"Hey," said Gregory Timberlake, "this

is the hour for boys and wenches to depart. You and I and Tom have graver matters to attend to."

"You'll have to drink without me. I want to talk to Tamsin."

Toby picked up a lighted candle. Tamsin did not want to talk to anyone but was too bewildered to argue. They went through to a small room where she often retired to escape the carousals.

He set down the candlestick. It was deep twilight; the tiny flame hardly brushed the surface of the darkness, but Tamsin stayed outside its radius; leaning, half kneeling, against a chest in the window.

She said: "They can't be betrothed. It isn't possible. Servants and underlings invent these foolish rumours. And I dare say Simon got hold of the wrong end of the stick, he often does. I'll tell you one thing that's certain: Harcourt is not going to marry Lucy Howard."

"Then why are you so concerned about him?" enquired Toby.

After observing her more closely, he had conceded that Margery was right for once. Here was a girl who had been thoroughly schooled in love: there was a difference in the way she carried herself, in the awareness of her eyes; even the shape of her mouth seemed to have changed. He had no right to object because she had chosen that dazzling young man to be her schoolmaster. What angered him was the thought that Harcourt could disillusion her so quickly, and that when it came to the point Tamsin was as pitiful as all the other girls who allowed themselves to be led astray. She should have had too much pride to complain, as well as too much sense.

She did not answer his question. He saw her outlined against the dusk, as though she had been cut in a cameo. A beautiful moth flopped in at the window, and then tried to get out again through a pane of glass, wings battering with fright.

"You aren't living in a fairy-tale," he said. "Whatever poetical nonsense Harcourt may have poured into your ears, you ought to know that a man in his position will be paired off with a suitable bride as early as possible. That's not to say he doesn't like you better than his little heiress. He might even continue to like you best, if you play your cards right."

"Who told you that I was his mistress? I suppose it was Margery. Well, you are both wrong."

She paused expectantly, waiting for him to challenge her. When he did not speak, she came out rather defensively with her announcement; she couldn't keep quiet any longer; it had become imperative to talk to someone.

"John Harcourt isn't my lover. He's my husband. We've been married since the beginning of June."

"Oh, my God!" muttered Toby.

"And what does that signify?" She turned her head slightly.

It signified Toby's black forebodings as he gathered how completely she had let herself be duped. It seemed cruel to awaken her — but more cruel to let her go on drifting in ignorance.

"Tell me about this marriage," he prompted her. "Where did it take place?"

"Here, in the parish church." Did he think she was green enough to be fobbed off with a private exchange of promises? She told him the true facts with some spirit. "We were properly married by a clergyman, according to the Prayer Book rite, and in front of two witnesses."

"I see. Can you prove it?"

"To be sure," she said. "John thinks we may find ourselves in trouble with the lawyers because we are both under age, but there can be no difficulty in proving that the marriage did indeed take place. Why should there be?"

"You had no banns called. And no licence from the Bishop?"

"I told you, we are both minors — "

"So you couldn't appeal to the vicar either. How did you come by your parson?"

"John got hold of him. His name was Blake, a very dignified, reverend sort of man; he is not able to accept a living on account of some conscientious scruple or other, I don't know precisely what."

"I could tell you where his conscience ought to pinch," said Toby cryptically. "What did you do for witnesses?"

"Mr. Blake brought one of them with him. The other was Giles Brown, who is

John's gentleman-in-waiting, though he's more of a friend than a servant. They were brought up together."

Toby was lost for words. Did she still not see the trap she had walked into?

"I don't think you have adequate proof," he said slowly. "If your story met with a denial, you could not produce a single witness on your side."

"What do you mean?" She stared at him, uncomprehending. "John knows where to reach Mr. Blake, and if we have any opposition from Sir Bernard — "

"It's not Kettering you have to fear. Can't you understand, Tamsin? There's one man who can make this entire history sound like a pack of lies, and that's Harcourt himself. If he says he never married you, then you haven't the slightest chance of convincing anyone."

"But he wouldn't!" she burst out. "John wouldn't do such a wicked thing, you must be mad to suggest it. John loves me."

"Then why are you so disturbed by these conjectures about Lucy Howard?"

She bit her lip. "He's living as a bachelor; he cannot avoid a certain measure of deceit. That little Lucy is the one who may be hurt."

"How chivalrous of you to care."

"Oh, be damned to you, Toby! I didn't think you could be so malicious. Why are you trying to poison my mind against John? What harm has he ever done you?"

Stolen my girl, thought Toby ironically, and it hasn't even dawned on her that I am jealous. She had forgotten everything outside her absorption with Harcourt.

There was still no reason why she should accuse him of malice.

"Judge the facts as I have seen them," he told her. "When I left in April, Harcourt was doing his utmost to lure you into bed with him. In June you were secretly married, without banns or licence, by a parson you can't trace, in the presence of one witness who vanished with the parson and another who regards Harcourt as his feudal overlord. And now, in August, your bridegroom has already ceased to visit you and is gallivanting around the country-side with a girl of his own station, while their families discuss her dowry.

What do you expect anyone to make of that?"

"He wouldn't break his word. He's a man of honour, a gentleman — "

"He's a nobleman." Toby made the cynical correction. "They are a law unto themselves. You wouldn't be the first young woman who was cozened into a false marriage by one of that fraternity. Do you know what happened to the Earl of Leicester's second wife?"

"She fell downstairs, and people said he pushed her. I don't see the relevance."

"That was his first wife. After she died, he was secretly married to the widow of Lord Sheffield and got her with child, but when she claimed to be his countess, he disowned her, and swore she was no better than a strumpet. And since she hadn't a scrap of evidence, he was able to be rid of her, and their son was declared a bastard. And you must have heard how the Earl of Essex let his wife's pregnancy become an open scandal before he decided to acknowledge her. She could do nothing but hide in her mother's house and await his pleasure."

"Essex and Leicester were both afraid

of offending the Queen. John isn't a royal favourite."

"I wasn't drawing an exact comparison, I was begging you not to pin too much faith on the safeguards you think you have obtained by your marriage. They don't exist. Douglas Sheffield was the daughter of one great lord and the widow of another; Lady Essex was the daughter of a Secretary of State and the widow of Sir Philip Sidney; if women of that degree can find themselves in danger of being cast off without redress, what do you suppose is likely to become of you?"

There was a long pause before she replied.

"All these tales may be true, but you are a long way wide of the target. John hasn't deserted me. It's my own fault that he hasn't been near me lately. We quarrelled — as all lovers quarrel — and I was very unkind to him. He is paying these attentions to Lucy Howard merely to punish me for that."

She spoke bravely, but her voice trembled. Toby felt he was acting like a brute; what was the good of warning her when it was too late and the damage was done?

"If I were you," he said, "I should smooth out your differences as soon as you can. And when all is well again, seize on a chance of talking freely to Lord Harcourt about your marriage and ask him whether there is any written record of it."

"Yes, I'll do that."

She did not say that she had already tried unsuccessfully to patch up the quarrel, nor did she explain what had set it off in the first place: John's strange lack of enthusiasm for the prospect of coming out into the open and admitting that she was his wife.

★ ★ ★

Toby and Simon were going to the play, and when they asked her to join them Tamsin accepted, though she was not in the mood for merrymaking. She hoped she might meet John.

The players had improvised a theatre in the enclosed yard behind the White Swan; they had a wagon which they used for a stage, and it was drawn up against the back of the inn just by the outside stairway, so that they could overflow into the gallery as well.

Tamsin craned hopefully through the crowd. There was not a sign of anyone from Minton Gabriel; perhaps no one at the great house thought it worth coming to see a quite undistinguished company which had been ambling around the neighbourhood all the summer. They would be accustomed to fine London actors with proper theatres on Bankside.

The citizens of Gaultonsbury were not so critical. They came pouring into the yard and stood in a tightly-packed throng, gazing expectantly at the stage, and shoving to get a little nearer. Between the main bulk of the audience and the wagon were some rows of benches for people of the better sort who had paid more so that they could sit down.

Toby captured three places for them, and started talking to someone in the row ahead.

"They've changed the play," he told Tamsin presently. "When I came through here yesterday they were planning to put on a comedy with some excellent fooling in it, but now they are performing a tragedy instead."

Simon, rather downcast, asked whether there would be any corpses.

"Four deaths on the stage, as far as I recall."

"So you have seen the piece before?" said Tamsin. "Is it very bad?" She realised that he was put out by the alteration.

"The original was well enough. I don't know what the pirates will have made of it."

"Pirates?" asked Simon hopefully.

Toby laughed. "Theatrical pirates. This play belongs by rights to the Lord Chamberlain's Men, because it was written for them by a member of their own company. They'd never allow it to be published — why should they? So along comes a pirate publisher and sends a clerk into the theatre to take down the whole piece in shorthand, and after it's been printed, anyone can read or perform it without benefit to the author."

Simon wondered what would happen if they caught the shorthand writer. Toby told him, two more people squashed into their row, and a girl came round selling ripe plums. Some of the audience began to stamp their feet impatiently.

The noise died away as a man playing the part of Chorus came forward to announce the Tragedy of Romeo and Juliet.

There was a fight near the beginning which pleased Simon, a series of encounters in the public street, and then a scene between the heroine, her mother and her nurse. After that a masque. Tamsin had realised by now why Toby had been disconcerted when he heard what play they were going to see. This was the story of a boy and girl whose desperate, secret love had to be hidden from their families; it was just a little too near home.

After the masque, Romeo climbed the wall into the Capulets' garden, and Juliet leaned out of her window and talked with him. The wooden gallery made a realistic setting for this long love-scene, and as it progressed Tamsin became enthralled, in spite of herself, the young couple seemed so real, and she heard everything they said with the heightened sympathy of recognition, like a traveller passing the land-marks on a familiar road. The boy so vehement, the girl afraid to believe too much. Rushing to the other extreme, giving herself away — and then wondering if he thought badly of her because she had been so unrestrained. The long-drawn-out partings, because neither could ever be ready to say good night. "I have forgot why I did call thee back." Oh yes, acknowledged Tamsin, that is exactly how it is with me and John. She had almost forgotten the quarrel, and that it was eight days since she and John had met secretly at night, like these lovers in the play.

The scene ended with Romeo going off to his ghostly father's cell, and immediately a black-robed figure appeared from behind the staircase at the back of the stage, saying something about the grey-eyed morn, so now it was day apparently, and this must be Romeo's confessor.

His face was partly hidden by his cowl, but there was an oddly familiar ring to the grave, sonorous voice. Tamsin was sure she had come across him somewhere, not long ago. She was just on the point of remembering where when he turned directly towards the audience, so that the whole appalling weight of the shock struck her through two senses at once. She saw and heard, without any loophole of a doubt, an actor she had admired in the part of a clergyman once before — he had been calling himself the Reverend Mr. Blake when he went through the form of marrying her to John in Sutleigh Parish Church.

"It's not true!" she protested aloud.

She had got to her feet without knowing. Several people hissed at her to sit down, and someone said the poor young lady was fainting from the heat. Tamsin was not fainting. She was painfully conscious of that white-haired dignified old man reciting his soliloquy in the tone she had found so moving at her wedding. Only it hadn't been her wedding. She was immediately and dreadfully aware of all the implications. Her body seemed to be divorced from her mind, so that she simply obeyed an instinct to get away and hide, stumbling over Toby's feet, and Simon's, as she tried to push past them to the end of the row. Toby got up and helped her out. Taking her arm, he forced a lane through the wedged mass of the crowd, and guided her into the tavern by a side door. Simon followed them, frightened that Tamsin was ill, but leaving with a longing glance at the wagon, where Friar Laurence had been joined by Romeo.

Toby led her into one of the dark little parlours, which was empty because everyone was watching the play.

"Now tell me," he said. "What's the matter?"

Tamsin sank on to the nearest settle. Her heart was kicking like a mule inside her chest, so that it was difficult to speak properly.

"You were right," she whispered.

"Right?"

"Save in one particular. You said I'd never find the parson again."

Toby did not need a lot of explanation. "Do you mean to tell me he employed Treves?"

"The one out there now, dressed as a priest. John said his name was Blake."

"That's Sam Treves. He's been in the

273

company for years playing the sober-sided parts, dukes and archbishops ... By Judas, what a villain the fellow is!"

It was not clear whether he was alluding to Sam Treves or to the man who had bribed him to perform a false marriage with such a convincing air.

"How could he do it?" Tamsin started to cry. "How could he be so cruel? To make those promises, knowing all the while what I should suffer when I found him out."

Simon hovered at Toby's elbow.

"Do you understand what she is saying?" he enquired anxiously. "Who is it that has hurt her? What did they do?"

"Lord Harcourt persuaded her into love with him, and then deceived her with a false marriage; she had begun to doubt him already, and now she has proof."

"You must be mistaken — he would never do such a thing! He would never dishonour a girl like Tamsin. Besides, he scarcely knows her."

"He knows her better than you think, and a great deal better than you know him. My good Simon, do you go around half asleep? I hadn't been back at Sutleigh two hours before I discovered that everyone else in the house believed her to be Harcourt's mistress. They may have under-rated her, but they knew what to make of him. Never dishonour a girl like Tamsin — are you mad? Haven't you yet learnt how men commonly treat unprotected women? You aren't a child any longer. If you want your sister properly cared for, it's high time you took the matter in hand, for it's plain your father never will."

Toby hated seeing Tamsin in such distress, and vented his feelings on the nearest scapegoat, which happened to be Simon. The boy looked miserable, his world had turned upside down, his idol Harcourt had betrayed him in betraying Tamsin, and now Toby was hinting things about her position which it had been easier for a schoolboy to ignore.

"Surely my father will take notice of this," he said rather uncertainly.

Tamsin stopped crying long enough to announce that she wouldn't have her father told. There was nothing he could do, and she could not endure the maudlin uproar of him and Margery and old Timberlake and all their cronies being sorry for her.

Simon protested. "You ought to let them know the truth. You don't want them to go on thinking ill of you."

Tamsin stared at him through her tears. "They don't think ill of me, why should they? They think I judge these matters as they do. Oh God, I wish I could!"

★ ★ ★

She was writing to John. Unlike her last letter, which had been composed with infinite care, this one was being dashed down so fast that she kept stubbing the point of her quill. When she reached the bottom of a page she sanded it lavishly and could hardly wait for the ink to dry before turning over. She was releasing all the avenging furies of resentment and disgust that had begun to consume her from the moment Sam Treves stepped on to the stage at the White Swan.

False, cowardly dishonest and con- temptible — no epithet was too bad for him, though a good deal of her contempt was directed at herself for having been so easily deceived. She ought to have known what he was. Arrogant and vicious, he'd tried hard enough to seduce her, always with the assumption that she ought to consider it a privilege, and once, when he was drunk, he'd tried to rape her. What a simple-minded fool to believe that such a man would ever dream of marrying a girl in her position. She should have had too much pride to listen to him; she should have sent him packing. But no — she had lapped up his lies, fawned on him like a wretched little spaniel, and all the while he must have been laughing at her stupidity and conceit.

Even at the height of her rage, Tamsin had enough insight to know that this portrait of a stage villain was too far-fetched. Some of the adoring, star-scattered phrases had been sincere, in the sense that he had been so wild to take her to bed with him he was prepared to offer anything in exchange, including marriage. However, it must have been difficult to find a parson, and possibly the idea of hiring an actor to deputise might have been intended as a temporary arrangement. Perhaps John had thought he could put things right by marrying her properly later on.

This was no excuse. No one had the right to misdirect and pervert the free choice of another human creature, for any purpose whatever, and as for any good intentions he might have started out with, what were they worth, now he had got what he wanted from her and was openly courting Lucy Howard?

I'm glad I'm not married to him, thought Tamsin. She began a new paragraph by telling him so.

She had finished her letter when there came a tap on the door.

"Who's there?" She had shot the bolt against unwanted solicitude from Margery.

"'Tis Prudence, mistress. I've brought 'ee some broth."

Tamsin was going to say she didn't want any broth, when an idea struck her. She opened the door.

"Is Jem going over the hill tonight, do you know?"

"He do go most nights," said the little pink-cheeked maid.

Her brother Jem, who worked for the blacksmith, was keeping company with the daughter of one of Sir Bernard's gardeners.

"Will you run down to the forge and find him? You can tell Molly I've given you leave. Ask him to take this to the great house and deliver it to Lord Harcourt directly if he is able, or else to one of the servants."

She gave the letter to Prudence, who seemed sufficiently awestruck to remember exactly what she had been told.

When she had gone, Tamsin tried to drink a little of the broth, but she could hardly swallow it. She had nothing left to do except sit and brood. This empty room contained too many echoes and images; she could not bear to stay shut up here alone, nor could she endure the supper-party in the parlour. Presently she crept downstairs and out through the back door into the lane that led up over the dividing ridge into the neighbouring combe.

She climbed the steep hill because her feet took her that way by instinct. When she reached the saddle of land that rose between the two valleys, she stopped and surveyed the green summer world around her. She had just passed the secret lair in the bracken where John had asked her to marry him. (Had he been preparing to make a fool of her even then? She would never be certain.) Below her on that side lay the whole of Sutleigh: the chimneys of the manor breaking through the trees, and the leaking roof of that infernal tithe-barn; Abbotsleat, where she had danced with him at Charity Mulcaster's wedding . . . Just across the way, tiny and fore-shortened, was the church — she did not want to be reminded of the church, and turned again to face Minton. Immediately in front of her was the flat stretch of grass where she had watched him exercising the Barb . . . On her left, high against the skyline, was the enigmatic prong of Wilfred's Tower. Her eye traced the up and down odyssey through bushes and briars which she had forced John to make that hot May afternoon when she had ridden off and abandoned him on the top of the Tower. Well, he'd had his revenge. She could not see right down ahead of her into Minton, because of the angle of the ground, but she had it all clearly in her mind's eye. Somewhere down there, John was enjoying himself, not caring . . . She jerked her head up and glanced to her right where the lane ran along the ridge for a short distance before dropping down into the woods on the Minton side. She was quite close to the corner where she had met John and his cousins when they were maying, and just beyond that was the narrow place where he had frightened her so much by nearly riding into the quarry . . . The two combes were unrolled for her like a map, and it seemed to be a map of her own heart, stuck through with pins.

Her thoughts lingered on the quarry. If it came to the worst, if she found she had conceived a child, she could throw herself over the edge, certain that a few seconds later she would be dead. She was determined that no bastard son or daughter of hers should survive to repeat the pattern of her misery.

She swung round and ran in the opposite direction.

She plunged through the wood, forcing her way between stunted ash trees and hazel saplings, slamming back the branches, indifferent to her scratched arms and torn skirt. She was running at random, in a panic-driven flight from her own despair. Presently she began to flag, with a stitch in her side. All violent emotions dissipated for the time being, she knelt on the ground and lay down, her cheek pressed into a pillow of damp, springy moss. She stayed there, imprisoned in the inertia of grief.

★ ★ ★

She lay in her mossy refuge for over an hour. Somewhere in the world outside the August sun was setting, so that the green branches were gradually deadening into a colourless gloom, and the birds of the wood had stopped singing.

She raised her head and sat up. She was on the verge of one of those little glades where they had picked bluebells. She was trying to think sensibly with the outer edges of her mind, while avoiding the pain at the centre. She noticed that the ground was hard and she was thirsty: she still had not quite summoned the initiative to move when she heard footsteps coming from the direction of Sutleigh, and a voice shouting her name.

"Tamsin! Ta-amsin!"

Either Toby or Simon, she was not sure which. An hour earlier she would have sat tight and let them go on shouting; now she knew that this would be unwarrantably childish.

"Here!" she called.

There was a pause, as though the searcher was getting his bearings. Then the steps began again, a tall shadow slid across the tree-trunks, and there, twenty yards away from her, was John.

He was dressed in hunting green, hatless and dishevelled, with a scratch on his cheek, as though he had been ransacking the woods from end to end. He looked distraught.

"Don't you come near me," said Tamsin.

He came on, paying no attention.

She was not prepared for this. She had taken it for granted that his desertion was calculated and final. When she wrote to him, she had hoped to pierce through any cracks in his conscience that were still sensitive to shame, but she had not expected him to come chasing into the woods after her, to make a display of his remorse. It was too late, he had hurt her too much, and she did not want to hear a word of it.

"I wish you would leave me in peace, my lord. I have nothing more to say to you."

"I have a very great deal to say to you."

It took her a few seconds to realise that his extreme pallor and his shaking voice were not signs of contrition. He was in a deadly, white-hot rage.

He said: "How dare you write me that infernal letter."

This was too much. "I suppose I must not presume to reproach your lordship? Since I am not worthy of the honour of being your wife — "

"You brass-tongued harpy, you *are* my

wife. However much I may regret it."

"Oh, for pity's sake! What's the use of pretending? I tell you, I saw your parson, and he's nothing more than a common player called Sam Treves — "

"His name is Samuel Blake — "

"I saw him this afternoon — "

"I've known him since I was a child — "

"Strutting on the stage at the White Swan — "

"He used to be my grandmother's chaplain."

By now they were each trying to shout the other down, but his last remark was so extraordinary that it threw her out of her stride.

"He can't have been," she said, with a feeling that was curiously like dismay.

"He was. An ordained minister of religion who has never been unfrocked. The marriage was perfectly valid."

"No!" she whispered, so appalled by the implications that she actually wanted him to be lying.

John did not look as though he was lying. He towered over her, belligerent and scowling.

"Blake was the son of the old lady's treasurer," he said. "He left in a hurry when it was discovered that he'd been teaching the serving wenches a good deal else besides the catechism. My grandmother would not have him pursued and brought before the Bishop; she did not want to add to the distress of his family, and she was always a law unto herself. That's why he's still in Holy Orders — though I gather he's been making a living on the stage for the past seven years. I recognised him when I went to the play at Garth in April; I think the poor fellow was afraid I might denounce him. So when I sent for him to marry us, he could scarcely refuse. I don't know why I tell you this, for I'm sure you don't believe a word of it."

But she did believe him. It was not a story anyone would invent. Equally, it was not a story that anybody could possibly be expected to guess.

"How was I to know?" she burst out. "Why didn't you tell me the truth?"

"Because I was fool enough to wish you to be happy on your wedding day. You thought we had been blessed by the presence of a wise and spiritual clergyman, and I didn't want to take away that comfort from you. I hadn't many gifts I could bring you."

He couldn't explain any better than that. Like any very young man in love, he had wanted to offer his bride the moon and the stars, when in fact he couldn't provide her with a roof over her head or the freedom to call herself by his name. This was so galling that he had not been able to resist a few small opportunities for making her position seem more secure and conventional. Giles had warned him that he was running a fearful risk. And Giles, as usual, had been right.

John sat down on a tree-stump. A lock of his thick, dark hair fell across his forehead; he brushed it back, smearing the blood on his cheek.

"You ought to have told me," said Tamsin, who was now thoroughly on the defensive. "Can you wonder that I took our marriage for a counterfeit, after I saw Blake up there on that wagon? What else was I to think?"

And at that John turned on her and stripped her of every feeble shred of an excuse that she might use to bolster up her faltering confidence.

"I know what most wives would have thought in such a case. They'd have thought there was some kind of mistake or misunderstanding (as indeed there was) instead of rushing to be logical with such indecent haste. They'd have refused to believe their eyes and ears, decided that the actor must have a twin brother who was a clergyman, or fixed on some other harebrained coincidence. Surely any woman who loved her husband would stretch the facts to the utmost limit of folly rather than believe that he was the blackest villain unhung?"

"John, I never called you that — "

"No, you merely accused me of perjury, blasphemy and sacrilege."

"I know it was very wrong of me. I jumped to the conclusion — "

"Jumped! You fairly flew to your conclusions, didn't you? You never considered any alternative. You neither examined the evidence nor gave me a chance to explain. I don't blame you for not guessing the truth. No one could have done that without knowing Blake's previous history, and it's entirely my fault that you didn't know it. I regret the distress you must have felt when you saw him among the players. But that doesn't cancel what followed: your readiness to condemn me without a hearing, and the intemperance of your attack. You took it for granted that I had deliberately tricked and betrayed you — did it never occur to you that I might also have been Blake's dupe?"

Tamsin gazed at him in consternation. She had been so influenced by Toby's worldly wisdom that this idea had never crossed her mind, yet she saw now that it ought to have done, long before she gave way to her suspicions.

"Did it not strike you," he said, "that some clever rogue might have passed himself off as a clergyman merely to lay hands on the fee? Does this seem so unlikely? So much more unlikely than my debauching you under the cloak of a false marriage and then deserting you?"

"No," she said in a low, troubled voice. "It's far more likely, and I can't think why I was so slow-witted. My dear love, I am very sorry for being such a doubting Thomas, and I do beg your pardon. If I hadn't listened to Toby — "

"Toby! Have you been discussing me with that confounded gull-groper?"

His manner had been daunting before; now it was lethal. Tamsin eyed him apprehensively, and discovered that she was afraid of this stern young man who had convinced her that he was her lawful husband and, in the same process, turned into a stranger.

"How many more of your father's boon companions are in your confidence?" he enquired sharply.

"None of them — my lord. I never said a word to anyone until last night when Simon came back from the hunt and said there was talk of your being betrothed to Lucy Howard. I was a good deal disturbed, and that's when I let out the secret to Toby. I am sorry if you are displeased."

"My God, I think I have some excuse! Never mind the secrecy, it's your disloyalty I can't stomach. You had only to hear a schoolboy repeating some servants' gossip about my betrothal to Lucy, and you immediately acted as though it was true, and ran wailing about your ill-treatment to Toby Strange, of all people. It seems to me that you have very odd notions of how a married woman ought to conduct herself."

"I have given you cause to think so," she admitted humbly. "But you had not answered my letter — my first letter, when I asked whether you wished me to come to the assembly at the hunting-lodge. I begged you to forget our differences, but you never replied, and I didn't know which way to turn."

John drew a deep breath. "I didn't reply for a very good reason. I received both your letters together when I got back from the hunting-lodge three hours ago. I had already left Minton on Tuesday before your messenger arrived. I went up a day ahead of the main party, and stayed on a day longer. Simon could have told you that. You may not have known what to think about Blake or Lucy; as to why I didn't answer your letter, you had simply to ask your own brother where I was and he could have told you . . . "

"Oh," said Tamsin rather faintly.

In fact he had told her, more or less. She now remembered him saying that John had slept overnight at the hunting-lodge, but she had quite overlooked the significance of this when Simon went on to speak of Lucy Howard.

"It's all of a piece," said John. He got up and began pacing the little glade up and down. He was very angry and very bitter. "You never trusted me. You expected me to betray you in some fashion or other. You never forgot the way I behaved towards you when we first met; in your heart you never forgave me for having tried to make you my mistress. God knows, I wronged you, and I suffered days and nights of remorse after I discovered your true character. I might have spared myself the pains, for it now appears you consider me incapable of repentance, and that to you all sins of the same nature are equally black. I have openly pursued the daughters of the game, without pretending to be more righteous than I am — and you have such a low opinion of me that you think I would just as readily deceive an innocent girl by an action of the most coldblooded wickedness and treachery. How you must have hated me, under the surface all along."

"You know that isn't true!" she protested. "If I've been misguided you must know that it's partly because I love you so."

"Not in any language that I can understand. What kind of love can exist without respect or liking or mere affection? Don't tell me you felt any of those things. If you had, you could not have written me that letter."

They stared at each other, hurt and hostile. Tamsin felt he was being unduly harsh; couldn't he see that it was the stress of being too violently in love that had left her so vulnerable? But John maintained that no woman who truly loved her husband could so easily doubt his integrity.

She got to her feet. As she went to him across the tangle of leaves and grass, he watched her without a flicker of expression in those strangely dark blue eyes. When she was close enough to touch him, he stepped back abruptly, knocking her hand off his arm.

"Let me alone, madam. I am not in the mood for dalliance. You change your tune too quickly for me."

She felt her whole body shrinking from that pitiless rejection. The tears were pouring down her cheeks and she could do nothing to prevent them.

"I know I have deserved your anger, but don't punish me any more. I — I can't bear to be treated as your enemy, and as for hating you, how could that be true? If I hated you, why did I marry you?"

"I know very well why you married me."

"If you imagine I was after your title or your fortune — "

"Oh, I acquit you of that. It's what my family will say, and as usual they will be wrong. You married me," John informed her judicially, "because you had an inordinate desire to lie with me, and neither your caution nor your conscience would allow you to do so outside the bonds of marriage.

"I don't cavil at your demanding a wedding ring," he added, before she had time to protest. "Every unprotected woman must make her own terms. Only let us not confuse virtue with expediency. You have had what you wanted; I hope you will not consider the price too heavy. We are now yoked together like a pair of oxen at the plough until one of us dies. Which may not be for another forty years."

The silence which followed was bleak indeed. She had no doubt that he considered the price on his side had been far too heavy, and that he blamed her for their hasty marriage which he visibly regretted. A short while ago she had been wondering how she could live without John; now she wondered miserably what it was going to be like to live with him if he was already tired of her.

"One thing's certain," he said. "We can't go on as we are. From now on there will be no more deceit of any kind, we shall live together openly before the world. We'll set out for Laleham in the morning."

"Laleham?" she echoed.

This was Harcourt's ancestral castle, about sixty miles to the north, on the borders of Wales. She did not see how he could manage to take her there, though she was too crushed to say so. After a slight pause she did venture to ask, "Won't your cousin try to prevent us?"

"He's over on the other side of the county, inspecting levies. When he gets back and hears the news, he will certainly come after us. That is my concern. All that is required of your ladyship is that you remember you are my wife (however little you may like it) and try to behave yourself accordingly."

The moon had risen. In the milky radiance of the little clearing, she could see him plainly against the confusion of the surrounding darkness. Weary and disenchanted, he braced himself with a certain stoicism. "Come, I'll take you home. We can't afford to waste the night in argument, there's too much to be done. You must be ready to start at dawn."

He picked out a narrow path which led eventually into the lane, and so down into Sutleigh. Striding ahead of her, he did not trouble to look round, or to help her over the rough ground. He was much too angry to be chivalrous.

She was expected to follow him as though she had been his dog.

★ ★ ★

They were riding northwards on a Roman road that cut geometrically straight across a strange countryside. They had left the woods and combes behind, and the stone-built houses they passed were a colder grey, but the uplands were rich and green; great flocks of sheep grazed over them in tribes, like clouds drifting across the sky. And every village had its patchwork of farmland, where the wheat and barley stood breast-high, baking to a pale ripe gold in the harvest sunlight.

Tamsin was beside John at the head of their little cavalcade; it was ten o'clock in the morning and they had hardly exchanged a word since leaving Sutleigh in a heavy white haze six hours ago. It had been an odd sort of departure for a bride and bridegroom — though perhaps the oddest thing was the fact that her father got up at cockcrow, dead sober, to see them off.

He had been well pickled in sack the

night before when John stalked into the parlour, leading Tamsin by the arm and demanding a private interview. He had already been at the house once that evening, enquiring for her and kicking up a dust because she had gone out. Tom Grove was at cards with Margery, Toby and Mr. Timberlake; he did not want to be interrupted a second time.

"Take a hand with us, my dear lord, take a hand," he kept saying. Picking up a deck of cards he held it out with an expansive gesture; the cards slid through his fingers and showered on to the floor like leaves in an autumn gale.

"For heaven's sake, father!" said Tamsin, disgusted with him. "Can't you understand that Lord Harcourt wishes to speak with you privately."

"Don't see the sense in that. No secrets from my friends."

"In that case," said John, "you will have no objection to their knowing that I have married your daughter, and that I shall be taking her away tomorrow to my estates at Laleham."

"What's that you say?"

Mr. Grove leant on the table, owlishly

trying to focus John and Tamsin into his bloodshot gaze, while Margery squeaked excitedly in the background.

"I dare say this news may surprise you — "

"Wait!" said Grove.

He staggered over to the ewry board, scooped up a handful of water from the jug and splashed it over his head and neck, so that the drops quivered on his beard. "Ah, that's put me to rights." He shook himself like a spaniel getting out of a pond. "Did you indeed say you'd married the wench? I can scarcely believe it."

"You do her an injustice, sir," said John austerely.

His father-in-law immediately became tearful; declaring that he had failed in his duty, he was a prodigal and a runagate who had never been able to provide his poor motherless child with a dowry, and this (so he said) had been preying on his mind and hurrying him towards an early grave.

The situation was not much improved by Mr. Timberlake who made a pompous speech about John's grandfather, or by

Margery, who was longing for details and not at all reticent about asking.

John behaved extremely well. It was Tamsin who felt impatient and resentful. She suspected that his grave civility was nothing but a mask to hide his contempt. She considered the familiar scene: the wine-stains on the table-carpet, and the queasy smell of the tallow candles; the two old men fuddled with drink, and Margery, whose dyed hair and skin-tight satin bodice were both evidence of her trade. She felt ashamed of them all, and ashamed of herself for being so uncharitable.

There was one member of the party who had kept very quiet. As John went on talking to Mr. Grove, Toby edged nearer to Tamsin.

"How can this be? The fellow we saw this afternoon — "

"Is an ordained minister after all. John has known him for years. He is a man of no repute, but he is still a clergyman — and I ought to have guessed there was some such explanation. I wish to God I had never listened to your croaking!"

"If I misled you, I am sorry for it. You

are very fortunate, my dear. Though it is no more than you deserve."

"Mr. Strange!" said a cool voice behind them.

Toby turned quickly. "My lord?"

"I believe you have given Lady Harcourt plenty of counsel of one sort or another. You will understand that the case is altered. From now on it is for me to advise her. And also — to protect her from annoyance."

Or, in plain English: keep away from my wife, and don't presume on past favours. Toby's thin face darkened to a dusky red, and a muscle at the corner of his old duelling scar began to kick beneath the skin. But his answer was swiftly conciliating.

"I should not dream of encroaching on her ladyship. She will have no further need for my poor services. I hope your lordship will overlook any misapprehensions that may have arisen. I have been a faithful watchdog, my lord." He managed a shallow, unconvincing laugh. "Watchdogs are apt to bark at friend and foe alike."

John did not trouble to reply. His

victory was complete. He had won the girl they both wanted, he had gained a moral ascendancy by marrying her, which was more than Toby had ever offered to do. Toby would not venture to cross him, for both these reasons but chiefly because he would not risk offending a man who would one day be so immensely powerful. He had been in love with Tamsin, after his fashion, since she was fifteen. Now that she was Harcourt's property, he turned away from her without another glance, and began to sort out the cards that had been thrown on the table.

Tamsin had never felt more isolated in her life.

John took himself off to Minton, to prepare for the journey and write a letter to his guardian. Margery was disappointed in his leavetaking.

"He treats you so formally; I suppose that is how great lords and ladies are used to behave. He must be very different when you are alone?"

"Very different," said Tamsin drily.

She had gone to find Simon, and discovered that his room was empty; the servants said he had bolted his supper and slipped out, wearing his oldest clothes, directly afterwards. This probably meant that he had joined a rascally friend of his in the village on a poaching expedition. It was a schoolboy's means of forgetting his troubles. She had wanted to reassure him: as far as he was concerned, all was well. She was properly married, and his idol had behaved irreproachably.

In the morning he was still absent; she left messages for him with her father before she rode away into the unknown.

And now it was mid-morning and they had come a long way. She and John and six of his servants, all mounted, besides a couple of pack-horses, and the precious Barb who was being tenderly led by Jenkyn. Giles was there, and an elderly man called Finch who was John's groom of the chambers and kept muttering to himself in a state of high indignation.

Tamsin looked sideways at her husband. He was riding along with a loose rein, preoccupied. She dared not allow herself to imagine what he might be thinking.

She summoned the courage to ask: "Why are we going to Laleham?"

Then she wished she had kept her mouth shut, in case he crushed her curiosity with one of his more brutal snubs.

But he answered quite pleasantly. "Having told my guardian that we are married, I must back up my words by taking you to live in one of my own houses. This is a challenge; it's for him to make the next move."

"Yes, I understand that, but why did you choose Laleham? You have always spoken as though Crossingbourne was your true home."

"It's twice as far to go." There was no more to be said.

"They covered another mile in silence. Tamsin remembered another ride, on their wedding-day: the long, happy climb towards the hunting-lodge, singing Sweet Nightingale in a mood of unquestioning triumph.

The words had assumed a special significance for them. They rang through the interior recesses of her mind, and it was then that she began, for the first time, to attach a new and disagreeable meaning to them. For surely it was by copying the line of conduct laid down in songs like Sweet Nightingale that she had landed them both in the wretched plight they were in at present.

Those stories always followed the same outline. The man wanted to make love. The girl refused, though you could tell this was what she wanted too, the little hypocrite, for she hung about tantalising him into offering larger and larger bribes, until the besotted fool finally offered to marry her. Then the trap closed quickly. And soon to the church they did go — yes, indeed: without a moment's delay, so that heedless carnality could have its reward. No more's she afraid for to walk in the shade nor sit in those valleys below. As to whether they were well-matched in any other way, that was not worthy of mention. They might be the most ill-assorted couple on earth, yet the girl would still deserve praise, according to the philosophy of Sweet Nightingale, if she had goaded the man into marrying her before she graciously allowed him to gratify her own sensuality.

I didn't do that with John, she assured

herself hastily. We were in love, truly in love, at any rate I was — I still am. That made all the difference. Only John had told her that she did not know what the word meant, and suppose he was right? Had she ever honestly loved him as a man, or had she merely desired him as a lover? Had she deluded herself into seeing him in a haze of glory, as a paragon of all the virtues, because she wanted her entirely natural longings to seem a great deal more high-minded than they were? Her vision of the paragon had certainly melted far too rapidly, directly things began to go wrong. Could love have been so faithless?

She dared not look at him, but there was no need to look, she had him by heart: that long, slim young man with his splendid shoulders and his princely carriage, the dark hair curling close to his head, the smoky blue eyes that were at times so sullen, and at other times so sparkling with light and gaiety that his briefest glance could make your heart swim. That was how she had seen him first in the courtyard of the White Swan, a predator intent on mischief. If her love had been born of that instant, how could she pretend that it was anything more than an enslavement of the blood? And the events of the last few days had so bludgeoned her sensibilities that it was impossible for her to recognise what she felt for him now. She simply knew that she ought not to have used her body as a bait for dragging life-long promises out of a boy of nineteen.

The sun rose higher, the roads were scorching and dusty and shadeless. At about midday they halted at an indifferent wayside inn, where Tamsin was served with some salted fish that made her thirsty all the afternoon. John did not come in with her, he stayed outside with his men. They were soon back in the saddle.

As the hours dragged on, she became more and more weary. This was the longest unbroken journey she had ever made, and she had started after a sleepless night, in a state of terrible strain and distress. By seven in the evening every muscle was aching, and she had to hold on to the pummel to keep herself upright. John, tireless as ever, was wrapped in his own meditations and seemed to have forgotten she was there.

They reached the top of a small rise, and a murmur of satisfied achievement ran through the party.

"There it is — at last!"

Tamsin blinked and raised her head. In front of them lay what appeared to be a walled city: an immensely high and varied range of buildings, stretched along the bank of a river and girded by a great perimeter of stone.

"Is that Laleham?" she asked stupidly. "I didn't know it was such a fine town."

John said: "You can't see the town from here; it's out of sight beyond those trees. That's the Castle."

Tamsin gazed in awestruck silence, overwhelmed by so much might and masonry. She had formed some idea of the wonders of Crossingbourne, which must be a grander version of Minton Gabriel; she had not, until now, considered John as a feudal baron living part of his life in his own armed fortress.

Laleham Castle was moated on the landward side through a conduit of water that was diverted from the river. The drawbridge was down, in these peaceful times, though the huge iron-studded gates were shut. They rode on to the bridge, and one of the grooms dismounted and knocked loudly on the gate.

Nothing happened.

The man banged again, the others craned their necks, gazing upwards at the ramparts, but there was no one in sight.

"They don't keep a very good watch," said Giles.

"They don't keep a watch at all. And where's the porter?" John was furious. He said stiffly to Tamsin, "I regret that you should be kept waiting, madam, because my servants are so dilatory."

"It's of no consequence, my lord."

"It is of consequence to me." He made a trumpet of his hands and bellowed. "Wake up, you cowardly slugs! The Spaniards have landed!"

This did provoke some response. A barely visible head bobbed up at one of the window-slits of the gate-house turret, and an aggrieved voice complained: "You've no call to go about insulting decent folks and telling fairy-tales."

"Fetch Captain Lloyd," snapped John.

"In good time, in good time. Who is it that wants him?"

"If you don't know who I am, I suggest you get Captain Lloyd to tell you, and that right quickly."

There was some uncertain muttering at the window after this, and another voice said, "Good grief, it's the young lord! Here, you run and get Mr. Wilby and the Captain, while I open the gate."

The heavy gate was so firmly bolted that it took an interminable time to open, and when it was finally thrown back the two principal denizens of the Castle had arrived to greet them: Mr. Wilby, the steward, a plump, friendly person, and a little lame Welshman who looked like a professional soldier — Evan Lloyd, Captain of the small company of men who kept the place in repair.

They were both apologising profusely.

"We received no message, had no idea that your lordship was arriving — "

"And that's a confession of idleness if ever there was one. You have mortified me in front of my wife, and kept her waiting on her own doorstep."

"Did your lordship say — your wife?"

echoed the steward.

They had been too overcome to notice Tamsin; now they surveyed her in astonishment.

Tamsin scarcely knew how to endure their scrutiny. It was cold and gloomy inside the walls of Laleham, where the sun never reached for longer than an hour at midday. The whole place oppressed her dreadfully: the blank, cliff-like faces of the buildings, the squat archways, the narrow, grim keep. Some of the men-at-arms were loitering about, staring at her — she thought they were men-at-arms, though in fact they were merely retainers wearing the crimson Harcourt livery. As for Lloyd and Wilby, it was easy to guess what they must be thinking of a bride whom their master had bundled in so unceremoniously, with all her stuff in a couple of cloak bags, and not a solitary maidservant to attend her. She saw their deep apprehension, and tried to smile at them — it was a hesitant and pleading smile, and it went straight to George Wilby's heart.

"We are honoured to welcome your ladyship," he began. His thoughts had been running exactly the way Tamsin suspected, but when she appealed to him through the eyes of a frightened child, he felt convinced that this beautiful girl had no vice in her, and that the story of her marriage to his master could not be so disastrous after all.

His speech of welcome became slightly involved, but much warmer than formality demanded. John looked at him sharply, but decided that he was perfectly sincere.

"I suppose it must be plain to you that we stand in need of all your good wishes. We were married secretly, without the consent of either of our families, and have come up here to weather the storm. We shall have Sir Bernard hammering on the gates tomorrow."

"Then this time, by God, we can be deaf in a worthy cause," said Evan Lloyd, anxious to make amends for their previous lapse. "Is it your lordship's intention to keep him out? I think I could raise the drawbridge, though the chains is a little rusty, whateffer."

John said he did not think their troubles could be settled by a full-scale siege. He sounded rather regretful.

* * *

Tamsin slept that night alone in the state bedchamber, in a gigantic bed that bore its bellowing draperies like a galleon in full sail. The room had been got ready for her in a hurry; if there were any deficiencies she was too tired to care. She slept for ten hours without stirring, and woke to find Mrs. Mary Morgan pulling back the curtains and asking whether her ladyship was ready to get up.

Mrs. Morgan was the steward's widowed daughter, a pleasant young woman who had been delegated to wait on Tamsin until some other arrangement could be made. There were also several little maid-servants trotting about with jugs and basins.

Tamsin asked, "What o'clock is it?"

"A few minutes after eight, my lady."

She had slept so long that she felt saturated with sleep. By the time she had washed in scented rose-water, and dried herself on a linen towel embroidered with coronets, the drugged sensation was wearing off, and she was embarrassed by the presence of a gaggle of women who were expecting to dress her as though she was a doll. Then she grasped the fact that these particular women were equally embarrassed; they were none of them trained to attend on great ladies and did not know precisely what to do. Tacitly they reached a compromise. Tamsin was left to dress herself in peace, while the servants set out an imposing breakfast: four or five kinds of meat, with ale and bread, relish and spices. All the plates and dishes were made of solid silver.

She noticed that they had laid two places. Did this mean that John was going to join her? She did not know what had become of him in this alien world, nor where he had spent the night, and she could not bring herself to ask.

She had just finished doing her hair when there was a rap on the door. One of the maids went to open it, and Tamsin heard John's voice outside.

"Will you ask her ladyship if she is ready to receive me?"

"Come in, my lord," she called to him thankfully.

John came in. He was wearing a green doublet, and one of the new falling-collars of white lawn which were becoming more fashionable than ruffs. There was an air of quiet elegance; he had somehow begun to look much older than the boy she had first known in April. They eyed each other across an invisible palisade of gravity and constraint.

"I hope you are well rested, madam." He turned to Mrs. Morgan. "There's no need for you to stay, Mary. I will serve Lady Harcourt myself."

The women curtsied and withdrew. John picked up a knife and advanced on the rare, red sirloin of beef.

When they were both seated at the table, he asked her again how she had slept.

"Passing well, I thank you, my lord."

"You were so tired last night, I thought you would prefer to be left alone."

"That was very kind of you. I hope it was not inconvenient."

"What the devil do you mean by that?"

Tamsin flushed. "I did not know — I was wondering if you could find anywhere to sleep."

Considering the size of Laleham Castle, this sounded exceptionally stupid. It was mortifying to be reduced to such a state of imbecility.

John merely said, "I have separate apartments of my own. It is customary."

It would be, she thought. One of the conditions of his life that she had not foreseen. She was beginning to realise how isolated a nobleman's wife might be, in certain circumstances. Without close friends or household duties, surrounded by every comfort, except the comfort of being either loved or needed.

She forced herself to eat a little beef, and crumbled her manchet of bread. The room was so still that she could hear the menservants' footsteps in the hall below. Though surely that was rather odd? How did the sound travel through the density of the stone? John's grandfather had made this part of the Castle habitable by quarrying a fairly light and spacious dwelling out of one side of the inner stronghold, but the thirteenth century walls remained; they were about eight feet thick. She glanced around her, puzzled.

John was watching her. "What's the matter?"

"I was trying to make out where the

sound is coming from."

"I'll show you."

The room was draped with costly hangings, now rather faded. On the wall behind the bed, and quite high up, a square of tapestry had been cut away to reveal a painted panel; Tamsin thought it was the door of a cupboard. John strolled across to open it, and it was not a cupboard after all, but an interior window with a view straight down into the great hall of the Castle.

"Oh," said Tamsin.

She went over to look. From this angle the hall seemed immensely long and deep, with the grey flagstones leading up to an ornate oak screen, where the Harcourt unicorn pranced heraldically in a forest of wooden lilies and roses. The echoing footsteps continued, as a couple of liveried retainers passed through into the courtyard, and then Giles appeared, talking to the steward. He paused to fondle the brindled head of an old dog who lay stretched in front of the empty hearth. An observer up here would soon have a shrewd notion of anything that was happening in the Castle.

"What a clever device."

"The Master's Eye," said John.

"Is that what it's called?"

Standing beside him, enjoying the puppet-show below them, she felt much easier with him. He was being a great deal kinder to her this morning.

He moved back to the table and poured himself a mug of ale.

"Tamsin."

"Yes?"

She turned, reluctantly, having caught a hardness of inflexion which suggested that something uncomfortable was going to be said.

"There are certain things I have to make plain to you. Sir Bernard is bound to arrive here before nightfall. When he comes, he will try to pretend that our marriage is illegal on account of all those small peccadilloes we reckoned with from the start — our being under age and so forth. I want you to remember that they were nothing but infringements of the civil law, and they cannot affect the nature of a religious marriage. Whatever my cousin may do or say, you are my wife, and death alone can divide us. Do you understand that?"

"Yes," she whispered.

He had some more instructions for her. "I dare say my cousin will ask you to leave us, so that he may talk with me privately. You are not to go. It won't be a pleasant encounter, and in the ordinary way I would sooner keep you out of it, but as things are I want you to hear every word that passes between me and Sir Bernard. Whatever happens, I won't have it appear that I deliberately betrayed you behind your back."

"I should never think so now." Her voice trembled on the edge of tears. "My lord, I am so ashamed of having doubted you. I would give anything in the world to set matters right between us. Only tell me what I must do."

He looked at her, and then away; his answer was bleakly uncompromising.

"Nothing that you can do will make any difference."

★ ★ ★

It was getting on towards supper-time when Giles stuck his head round the

319

door of the small parlour where John and Tamsin were sitting, and announced that a sentinel on the ramparts had sighted a party of travellers.

John was at one end of the table, propped on his elbows, reading *The Noble Art of Venery*.

He said, "For God's sake, see that damned Welshman doesn't raise the drawbridge. You and Wilby had better meet him at the gate, Giles, and conduct him to me here."

When Giles had gone, he returned to his book.

Tamsin was at the other end of the table. She sat up a little straighter, wishing she had something to occupy her hands.

Without lifting his eyes from Turberville, John told her to stop fidgeting. "Ten more minutes before you need to fret." He turned a page, and went on reading.

It was not until they heard the noise of horsemen in the court outside that he got up in a leisurely way and went to stand close to Tamsin, his hand resting lightly on the back of her chair.

They heard their visitor approaching

across the stone flags, and the well-known voice, rasping with impatience.

"You need not escort me; I don't require a herald."

The door opened. For a moment they all stared at each other. Bernard had ridden a long way under a parching sky. His boots were thick with dust. Weariness and irritation accentuated the decisive lines round his eyes and mouth. He slammed the door behind him and threw down his whip and gloves.

"Well, your May-games have ended." His acute anger was damped by the contemptuous disillusion of a man who has constantly to clear up the damage done by a recalcitrant child. "You will leave here separately tomorrow, and you will not meet again. Luckily Mr. Grove is willing to take his daughter back, in spite of this escapade. (Under the circumstances, he could hardly do otherwise.) As for you, my lord, you are going to spend the next six months in solitary confinement at Nunehead, while I get this sorry business put to rights, and try to undo the harm you have done."

He paused. John was breathing rather

fast, but he did not speak. Kettering addressed Tamsin with the civility of cold dislike.

"I must ask you to withdraw. I have certain things to say to Lord Harcourt which he would prefer to hear alone."

Tamsin looked at John.

He said: "Stay where you are."

"As you wish, my lord."

"On your head be it," said Kettering. "If you choose to be admonished in front of your paramour — "

John found his tongue. "You are not to call her by that filthy name — "

"It's one she must have grown used to by now."

This, for John, was the crossroads. There was a brief hesitation. Then he burst out: "I'll make you unsay that, you sneering devil," and launched himself on his guardian.

"John — no!"

Tamsin jumped up and seized his wrist. Clinging to him with both hands, she managed to thrust herself in front of him, so that he could not get at Sir Bernard without forcibly removing her first. He might very well do that, and she knew how rough he could be when he lost his temper, but it was her only hope of keeping them apart.

"Let him be," she said. "I beg you, my lord, don't quarrel with your cousin over what he says of me. I'm not worth it."

She had been leaning her whole weight against him. To her surprise and relief she felt him lift the pressure and give way. He looked down at her, for the first time since their estrangement, with an entirely free and untroubled gaze that had even a hint of amusement in it.

"I thought I told you not to interfere." He spoke quite gently.

"I'm sorry. I couldn't bear to be the cause of fighting and bloodshed. Will you promise me — "

"Go and sit down and behave yourself. Yes, very well — I promise. I won't hit him."

A marvellous thing had happened to John. In the grip of a fierce determination to defend Tamsin he had at last acquired the courage to stand up to his guardian. It was now possible to face Bernard as though he was an ordinary mortal and even to knock him down — only that was no longer necessary. He didn't need to prove his manhood by a display of physical strength. He knew that he was old enough and brave enough to fight the battle of wills which had now become inevitable. The spell was broken.

It was not like Bernard to stand by doing nothing while his ward decided whether or not to hit him. But Bernard, not taking John's histrionics very seriously, was more interested in this passage between him and the girl. He had come here to rescue a half-fledged libertine from the clutches of an ambitious and experienced wanton. This was not how the young couple struck him now. The bold and flashing Tamsin was quieter than he ever remembered her. Far from driving her accomplice on, she was trying to restrain him, though her manner was curiously deprecating; she actually seemed to be a good deal in awe of him.

Bernard had an unusual qualm of self-doubt, which vanished when John had the impudence to tell him, "I cannot allow you to abuse my wife."

"I am thankful to say that she is not your wife."

"I am surprised that you should boast of being thankful, cousin. According to you, we are living in sin."

"I had rather see you live in sin," retorted Bernard unwisely, "than married to this young woman."

John caught his breath. Tamsin made an impulsive movement reaching out her hand; she thought he was going to lose his temper again and fly at Sir Bernard's throat. But this time John had found a different method of attack.

"What a damned hypocrite you are," he remarked. "In spite of all your moralising piety. If there is one thing that has finally sickened me, and destroyed my belief in your judgment, and your claim to set me an example — I tell you, sir, it is the way you have acted towards Tamsin."

"The way I have acted!" echoed Bernard, unable to credit the heresy that John could find anything to criticise in him.

"You and my cousin Ann have always spoken of her as though she was a common strumpet, when as far as I can see you hadn't a tittle of reason for doing so except that she was poor and illegitimate. Oh yes, I know she has been considered too free in her deportment by all the headshaking matrons in your neighbourhood. Good God, what else did they expect from her, living in that bear-garden at Sutleigh? And where else did they expect her to live? What did they ever do to save her from the perils that surrounded her? What did you do? Tamsin was fourteen when her father brought her down to the West Country. The Mulcasters were kind to her from the start. The rest of you passed by on the other side. And then, having continually neglected her, you were displeased to find that she had the insolence to grow up so beautiful without asking leave of her betters, so you spread all manner of false reports about her, and I am ashamed to say that when I first met her, I believed them. I've no wish to unload my own folly on a scapegoat — yet I can't help remembering that I was misled in the first place by those who ought to have known better."

"Have you finished your homily?" enquired Bernard. The irony fell flat; he was too dumbfounded by this onslaught to think of anything further to say, which was fatal from his point of view, because John had not nearly finished, and he immediately began again.

"Leaving aside your malicious comments on my wife's virtue, I can see no reason why you should harangue us as though we were a pair of vagabonds brought up before your worship on the bench. You have no divine right to say whom I may marry. You are not my father. You were appointed by the Court of Wards to take charge of my affairs until I come of age: a viceroy, not a king — and you have assumed the pretensions of an usurper."

"Now, see here, Harcourt — "

"*Will* you listen to me!"

John slammed down his hand on the table so hard that the boards jumped; it must have hurt, for he glanced at his fingers with a vague astonishment. Bernard was apparently stupefied. He had never heard John speak in such a voice before. Tamsin had. She had heard it two nights ago in the wood: the voice of an essentially honest young man who had at last woken up to certain bitter truths about himself and his circumstances after the sheltered ease of a boyhood that had been far too prolonged.

"You have kept me in swaddling-bands," he said. "You have made me so dependent that I have never learnt to bear my own burdens. Whatever I think, you condemn my ideas out of hand, and you ascribe the basest motives to whatever I do. You surround me with petty prohibitions because it is your duty to guard me, and the cream of that jest is, you miss what goes on under your very nose. I got married two months ago and you never knew. I visited my wife almost every night and you never found out. You stopped me going to Sutleigh because you thought I went there to play cards! And by the same token, I don't think much of the way you set about curing me. Yet how should this concern you, after all? You don't care what becomes of me in the end. All you care for is that I should be a properly obedient ward so long as I am under your dominion. You have been an excellent guardian to your own self-esteem. You have nearly been the ruin of me."

After this there was a very long silence. Tamsin had been staring steadfastly at the ground ever since John had started talking about her. Now she took a quick glance at Sir Bernard, and was startled by what she saw. There was a leaden tinge under the surface of his skin, as though a physical blow had driven all the blood away from his heart. That last deliberate cruelty had shattered the fabric of a relationship which had existed, unquestioned, ever since John was a child.

All the same, Bernard was the first to come back to the matter in hand. Age and experience had taught him their particular lessons; it was possible to hurt him, much harder to deflect him from his purpose.

"It's as well," he said heavily, "that I am not required to satisfy your lordship's present humour. I am meant to protect you from your youthful mistakes, not to endorse them. Ten or twenty years from now, if you can look back and admit that I was right to extricate you from this one, then I shall not have completely failed in my duty."

He felt very tired. He had got home to Minton late last night, to find his household in an uproar, his wife in tears, and a letter from John for which he was totally unprepared. After a long day in the saddle he had been met at Laleham with a hostility that was almost hatred from the boy he had cared for like a son. John's attack had wounded him to the quick. Was it possible that he had misjudged Tamsin? No, of course that was ridiculous, he'd heard too many stories about her, and either way, what difference did it make? A penniless bastard could never be an acceptable bride for the fifteenth Baron Harcourt de Laleham.

"However you try to beg the question," he said, "the fact remains that you are not lawfully married, because you cannot marry without my consent. You have behaved in the most rash and ill-considered manner altogether. What sort of a reception do you think you are going to get from the Howards after the way you've treated Lucy? You won't be able to show your face in London for months to come. You have done yourself an immeasurable amount of harm, and if you think that brazen impudence is going to carry you through, you are quite mistaken."

John heard him in a mood of growing despondency. Not over the gloomy prophecies about his future, which he took with a grain of salt, but because it seemed as though his personal victory over his cousin would accomplish 'nothing. Bernard was still doggedly sticking to what he thought was his duty — and John calculated that if he and Tamsin were going to be forcibly separated for the next two years, all his hopes of happiness were ended.

It should not have been so. At eighteen and nineteen it should have been possible for them to possess their souls in lonely patience for two years. But he had spoilt everything by his childish impetuosity, his cowardice and his self-centred greed. No wonder Tamsin distrusted and despised him. What would she think of him now, if he allowed her to be carted ignominiously back to Sutleigh while his friends tried to obliterate all traces of their hole-and-corner marriage? She certainly wouldn't believe that he was capable of being faithful to her for two years, and once they had been parted, he did not think she would ever consent to live with him again. She had too much pride to return to a man she did not respect.

He had got to discover some way of changing Bernard's mind.

He was mustering his arguments when the door flew open, and Mr. Wilby burst in without ceremony, insisting that he must speak to his lordship.

"Get out!" said John, furious at being interrupted.

The steward stood his ground. "It is a matter of urgency, or I should not have disturbed your lordship otherwise. There's a young lad — a stranger — loose in the Castle who is threatening to kill you."

"Threatening to kill me?" repeated John, taken aback. "For what cause?"

"Without doubt he is mad."

"Then why was he let into the Castle?" asked Sir Bernard.

"Because we thought he was with you, sir," replied Wilby.

This was not well received, and he hurried to explain. The boy had arrived at the gate a short while after the main party, implying that he had been left behind at a wayside forge with a horse that had lost a shoe. So they had welcomed him in, but instead of joining Sir Bernard's servants he ran way, played a game of catch-as-catch-can all round the armoury, helped himself to a weapon, and made an impassioned speech that no one could properly understand. After which he had somehow given his pursuers the slip.

"What sort of a weapon?"

"One that proves him to be deranged. If he'd chosen a dagger or a cudgel there might have been some sense, but stealing a longbow and a quiver of arrows — "

"Was a great deal more astute than you think," said John. "For he certainly knows how to use them."

"Why, do you know who it is?" demanded Sir Bernard.

"I can guess." John appealed to Giles who had just come in with Captain Lloyd. "I suppose it's Simon?"

"Yes. Misinformed on every point and howling for revenge. I couldn't make any

333

headway with him."

John glanced sideways at Tamsin. "Does Simon think he has a good reason for killing me?"

"I don't know," she faltered unhappily. "He was with me at the play, and directly we got home he disappeared. It never dawned on me at the time, but I suppose he went off to look for you at the hunting-lodge . . . " Having missed John there, he might have followed him to Minton, and then let Sir Bernard lead him to Laleham. In which case he would never have got her message. "I am so sorry," she said, "I am afraid this is all my fault, but I can put matters right as soon as we find him."

"Lloyd and I will attend to that," said Sir Bernard. "You had better stay here. You too, Harcourt."

John paid no attention. He simply opened the door and stepped into the hall, with Tamsin, Bernard, Giles, Wilby and Lloyd close on his heels. Three serving-men had just come out of one of the other rooms, where they had been searching.

As they all trooped across the stone

flags, it struck Tamsin that they might spend hours hunting for Simon in this warren of buildings.

And at that very instant, so soon that they were unprepared, a disembodied voice floated above their heads and startled them all out of their wits.

"Stand, Lord Harcourt, do you hear me! Stay where you are or I'll shoot. And the rest of you keep still too, or I'll shoot him through the brain."

They halted in a confused huddle, and nine heads jerked comically upwards like so many puppets on the end of the same string.

"Simon!" exclaimed Tamsin.

He was looking down as she had looked that morning, from the interior window that John called the Master's Eye. Simon must have found it by chance when he was roaming through the private apartments and seized on the vantage point. They could see the dark square very high on the bare wall, with his head and shoulders dimly outlined in the shadows, his raised hand curling round an invisible bowstring. One thing they could make out plainly was the gleaming tip of an arrow that pointed straight at John.

"Simon, do put down that wretched bow and stop acting tragedies! You have no quarrel with Lord Harcourt. I know it's my fault for misleading you, but it was all a mistake, and if you'd had the sense to go home before chasing us all this way, my father would have told you — "

"I did go home. I had your message, but I'm not as easily taken in as you are. Can't you see the fellow's lying to you?" The indictment sounded strange in the newly-broken boy's voice, husky and unequal. "Ask him, then. Ask him to declare his purpose openly whether he means to honour his promises."

Tamsin said to John, "I wish you will put his mind at rest, or I'm afraid that arrow may hit someone by accident."

John had been thinking fast. He was sure there was an opportunity for him here, if only he could see how to use it. If Simon could be enlisted on his side — but that wouldn't work, he told himself: once he knows I married his sister in good faith, he'll stop wanting

336

to kill me. It was no good persuading Simon, he had got to be goaded.

So he spoke up with an affectation of callous mockery.

"My dear boy, it's a waste of time your playing Robin Hood with me. I'm in the happy position that I don't have to keep my own promises; my guardian will insist on breaking them for me. And if your sister didn't figure it out from the start, that's no fault of mine."

"Why, you cold-hearted villain!"

Simon's fingers tightened, Tamsin gave a small shriek of protest, and John jumped. He had over-played his part apparently. He had no idea that Simon would prove so malleable.

"Don't be a numbskull," he called out hastily. "I'm quite willing to stay with Tamsin; I don't care who my wife is, so long as my guardian will let me have some money. Try to convince him of that. You have a very pointed argument up there."

"What on earth's come over you?" demanded Tamsin, who could not understand why John had chosen this perverse moment for contradicting everything he had been saying for the past two days. Simon's expression was murderous. Once get an obsession into his head, and he was like a mad bull; she appreciated that, if no one else did. She tried to put matters right.

"Pay no attention to Harcourt. He is talking nonsense, (God knows why). I assure you, he is our best friend, no one could have been more loyal or more chivalrous — "

"Hold your tongue, you silly girl!" John hissed at her,

Bernard, who was behind them, began to reason with Simon in a tone of calming authority. Couldn't he see that his threats would get him nowhere? How would it help his sister's cause to shoot Lord Harcourt and get hanged for murder? If he came down quietly, he could trust them to see that her interests were properly protected.

"Protected from whom?" enquired John acidly.

Simon was not listening to any of them. Light-headed for want of food and sleep, he was still imprisoned in the mood of black despair that had come over him two days ago at the White Swan, when Toby Strange had made Tamsin's position brutally plain to him, and forced him to understand how she was regarded by men like Harcourt and Kettering. Tamsin was the only person who had truly loved Simon in all his life, the one safe rock in a fickle and shifting world. That these men could set out to hurt and disgrace her was an obscenity that choked him with rage and grief, and self-reproach too, because he hadn't taken better care of her. He rubbed the taut bowstring with his thumbnail, thinking: I've got to kill him. I've got to. I can't let anyone do this to Tamsin and live.

Sir Bernard had finished his harangue. There was an uncertain pause, and the little Welshman said, "He's feinting! He doesn't mean to shoot."

"Yes, I do!" retorted Simon. So they wouldn't take him seriously? He'd show the louts.

There was a sharp twang. Tamsin screamed. John ducked, in spite of himself. For a second they all thought that Simon had aimed at him and missed.

Until they turned and saw that the arrow had flown over their heads and was sticking out of the carved eye of the unicorn in the screen.

They gaped at it, and one of the servants gave a whistle of unwilling admiration. There was something very disagreeable about the way that shaft quivered in the wooden eyeball.

Bernard swung round. "Get away, John! Quick, before he can loose another!"

He was too late. Simon had already snatched up a fresh arrow and notched it into place. And John had not moved.

"There, I've shot you a fat buck." Simon's laugh had an edge of hysteria. "And this one's for his lordship. If you don't between you promise my sister her rights before I count ten, I'll serve him the same way. One . . . Two . . . "

I believe he means it, thought John, oddly detached. It was all a matter of whose nerve broke first, Simon's or Bernard's. He wasn't going to speak. Tamsin was crying out to him, imploring him to promise, to explain. But it was useless to start explaining now, and no one but Bernard could make the promise that would satisfy Simon. Never again, John decided, not even to save his life, would he make a promise that another man had the power to renounce for him later. In that instant of nervous exaltation he felt quite literally that he would rather die than let Bernard and Tamsin see him humiliated any further.

"Five . . . Six . . . "

Tamsin turned on Bernard. "How long are you going to stand there dumb, you bloody monster? Do you want to have John butchered to preserve your stinking pride?"

"Seven . . . Eight . . . "

Bernard saw they had beaten him, the two obstinate boys, separately indulging in their private heroics. He gave in.

"Very well, Simon. What do you want me to promise?"

"That you'll make sure my sister is lawfully married to Lord Harcourt, and treated with her proper consequence. Swear it."

"I swear it," said Kettering grimly.

Simon withdrew the arrow and vanished from the dark square of the window.

"After him, boys!" yelled Captain Lloyd.

"We'll have him now, the bastard!"

He didn't know how exactly the term fitted. He simply knew that he and all the other Laleham men had been intolerably shamed by the sight of their feudal lord at the mercy of that little grinning ape, who had made such fools of them, and they were spoiling for vengeance. They poured across the hall to the further door.

"No!" shouted John, running after them. "You're not to lay a finger on him!"

They all pushed through the door pell-mell and ran to the corner tower, where a spiral staircase led up to the state apartments. As they reached the bottom of the stairs, Simon was beginning to come down. When he saw the posse waiting for him he checked, missed a step, and fell headlong. He rolled over and over like a sack of turnips, and landed at John's feet.

★ ★ ★

"Could you have brought yourself to do it?" asked John.

"I don't know, my lord," muttered the

342

boy, shifting a little on the feather-bed. Painfully, because his bruises hurt, and also because he had now been given the whole story, and could hardly bear to face his brother-in-law. "I don't know."

They would none of them ever be certain, though John would always maintain that Simon could not possibly have shot him in cold blood, that he had known this all along, and that his own display of Roman stoicism had been just a piece of play-acting.

Simon had a sprained ankle and two cut knees. He had been bandaged, put to bed, and sustained with a large plate of venison pie, which Tamsin said he didn't deserve.

"Don't judge him too harshly," said John. "He was trying to help you and you should be grateful."

"So I might be, if he'd had any good reason for such antics, but why he didn't pay attention to what my father told him — I don't understand you, Simon. What possessed you?"

"If you must know, my father said that no one would recognise such a marriage, and of course Lord Harcourt knew it, but at least you had established a claim on him, and you were better off as a rich man's mistress than an old maid. Mark you, he was drunk by that time or he wouldn't have spoken so freely. I felt sick."

"Oh," said Tamsin, wishing herself at the bottom of the sea. She turned and walked out of the room.

She was standing in the gallery, struggling with her acute mortification, when she heard John come out behind her.

"I'm sorry," she said, without turning round. "There's not much to choose between any of the Groves, is there? I don't wonder that your cousin would almost prefer to see you dead than married to one of them."

"There's no call to distress yourself," he said equably. "After all, I've known what your father was from the start. And it's entirely due to him that Simon arrived here in a state of righteous wrath and settled our business for us. For don't you see, he's extracted a promise from Bernard that I should never have got on my own."

"You don't think he'll back out?"

"Break his word — Bernard? You must be mad."

"He might say it was a promise given under duress."

John laughed. "Do you suppose he'll ever admit that he let himself be worsted by a child of fifteen, and that he was obliged to sue for an amnesty on any terms? If he tried to wriggle out on that score, my servants and I could make the story known, and he'd never to able to hold up his head again. No, what's done is done; he'll accept matters with the best grace he can, you'll see."

And so it turned out. When they met at the supper-table a few minutes later, Sir Bernard had recovered his urbanity, and if he was non-committal as to her exact status, his manner towards her was exceedingly correct. So long as the servants waited on them, he and John kept up a flow of small talk. Tamsin was tongue-tied. She kept remembering how she had screeched at Sir Bernard and called him a bloody monster.

The last flagon of wine was set on the table. John gave an order and the servants withdrew. Now there must be some sort of reckoning. An ominous silence hung over them.

Examining the silver chasing on his goblet, Sir Bernard spoke at last. "It will be best if we return to Minton tomorrow."

"And Tamsin will come with us — as my wife?"

"Certainly. I should not ask my wife to receive her otherwise."

Tamsin pictured the welcome she was likely to get from that mealy-mouthed Ann Kettering.

John was making the most of his victory. "After that, if it please you, I should like to set up my own establishment at Crossingbourne."

"Yes, you may as well do so straight away. Under the circumstances."

Having made this concession, Sir Bernard set down his cup, cleared his throat, and glanced at John with a curious expression that Tamsin could not at first identify. Then she realised that it was apprehension.

"There is one matter," he said, speaking quickly and rather low, "that

I should prefer to settle while you are at Minton; I think we should arrange for the vicar to perform a private marriage ceremony — "

"By God, I have borne enough!" John thrust back his chair and stood up, his voice was a semi-tone deeper than usual and shaking with rage. "If you are still harping on that same tune — "

"My dear lord, don't lose your temper again," Tamsin implored him. She saw Sir Bernard was looking desperate; he too had come up against John's hidden seam of iron, and she was sorry for him. "Won't you at least listen to what your cousin is trying to suggest?"

To her surprise, he did what she asked, though with a good deal of suspicion. "Go on," he said to Kettering. "Tell me why you think we need a further ceremony."

"Purely to safeguard Lady Harcourt."

It was the first time he had used that name, and John was slightly pacified. "Go on," he said again.

"I hope the need may never arise. As long as you live, I doubt if it will. But suppose you were to die, leaving her with

347

children too young to fight their own battles? I have a strong suspicion those bloodsucking Harcourts at Yateley would lay claim to the title on the grounds that you were never properly married and had left no direct heir. And if your various evasions of the law were judged too strictly by the letter, your widow and children might be disinherited.

"I wish you will attend to this, John." Bernard leant on the table, speaking with obvious difficulty. "I seem to have failed completely in all I have tried to do for you, and you apparently think you have good reason to hate me, but I do have your welfare very much at heart, and I should be sorry if your distrust of me led you to reject the advice I am trying to give you now. And perhaps to injure the one person you most want to protect. I have said I will recognise your marriage, and as far as I am concerned that means I now have a duty towards you both."

John had been fidgeting uncomfortably during this painful re-opening of old wounds. He spoke to Tamsin. "How do you say? Would you prefer another wedding?"

Although she had decided that she would much prefer it, she had acquired enough finesse to avoid hurting his pride.

"It is for you to arrange matters as you think fit. I will do whatever your lordship pleases."

"Very well, I will consider the question," said John with an air of casual grandeur.

He could now afford to give in and accept Bernard's advice. Honour was satisfied.

Tamsin caught Bernard's eye, and in it a gleam of unmistakeable admiration.

Soon afterwards John escorted him to his bedchamber. Once again the Castle servants had been called on to provide a lodging at short notice.

"I am afraid this chamber is not as well appointed as it ought to be." John was playing the punctilious host.

"It will suffice." Bernard glanced round the bleak room without really seeing it. "Harcourt, I think I owe you an apology."

"You owe me what?" John could hardly believe his ears. Now that he recalled some of the things he had said before supper, he thought the boot was very much on the other foot.

"I can see that I must have appeared to you as the most intolerable and senseless tyrant. And all with the best intentions, I assure you. The truth is that you were always so spoilt and indulged by everyone else, that I tried to redress the balance. Where others were too lenient, I felt obliged to be deliberately and often unduly severe. It sounds logical, doesn't it? But of course it was nothing of the kind; I see that now. While you were a child it was easy, but lately I'm afraid I must have done you more harm than good. I'm sorry, John."

"You are too generous, sir."

He was amazed by that generosity. It took a man of great integrity to be capable of such a response. He found the old, unwilling respect returning in an altered form.

"I know I've been uncivil and ungrateful," he muttered. "I wouldn't have spoken in such extravagant terms, only you were trying to separate me from Tamsin — "

"Ah, Tamsin! My blackest crimes were committed against her, is it not so?"

John was not sure whether he was being serious or ironic.

He said: "I know you cannot share my opinion of her. When you come to understand her better — "

"I think I have come to understand her pretty well. No, don't fly into a passion; I mean that in all good faith. I have watched you together, and I can see that it is not what I first thought. Besides, something must have converted you into a champion of virtue, you were not much inclined that way three months ago, and I think only an encounter with true innocence could work such a transformation."

"Yes, you are right. She has changed my entire life. She is so good, she is an angel — "

"She is a remarkable young woman, and I hope she'll be able to rise above her family. When I think that the next Lord Harcourt is going to be a grandchild of that drunken sot, and on the wrong side of the blanket into the bargain — I should think your father must be turning in his grave! However, I will say that neither Tamsin nor Simon takes after Tom Grove. Not that a would-be murderer is much to boast of, and heaven knows what the boy will grow up into. At least he's only her half-brother."

"But they are very dear to each other, and he certainly ought not to be left at Sutleigh. We shall have to take him with us to Crossingbourne."

John looked rather warily at his cousin as he said this, for no matter how much he might have mellowed, Bernard was still his guardian, and could hardly be expected to encourage such a scheme. But Bernard, after reflecting for a moment, merely said he thought it would be a sensible arrangement.

"You do?"

"If you set about it properly. You should give him the run of the house at all seasons, make him free to live within your family circle, spend a great deal of time and care on his education, and a great deal more rescuing him from all the pitfalls he is bound to stumble into — and a few years from now, if you are lucky, he will turn on you as though you were his worst enemy, and tell you that you have ruined his life, all for the sake of your own self-aggrandisement."

"For God's sake, sir — you are making me feel the most loathsome viper that ever crawled under a stone! I wasn't — I didn't — it surely can't have sounded so bad as that?"

"My dear John, I am simply warning you of some of the pleasures in store for you; the temptation was irresistible. You were not meant to take them to heart."

It had been necessary that the memory of their violent clash should be quickly cauterised with laughter. Now that was done, it need not be mentioned again: forgiven and forgotten on both sides, in theory at any rate. If Bernard continued to be haunted by a sense of mortification and failure, there was no reason, he decided, why John should ever know.

"Go back to your bride," he said, smiling. "I have no business to keep you dawdling here. And she has earned the right to enjoy your society: she has done more to make a man of you in five months than I could achieve in twelve years."

So John went back to Tamsin, slowly, because he had a guilty conscience. He might never understand how much he had hurt Bernard: he was not oblivious here. The servants had cleared the supper-table, but Tamsin was alone, sitting on a seat against the wall, in the parlour, so still that she could have been carved out of alabaster. There was something proud and forlorn about her profile that filled John with an aching compunction.

"Don't be so sad," he told her. "We have made a wretched start, but from now on everything will be changed. I will make up for the past, I promise you."

"You have done that already." Her voice was almost inaudible, "I shall never forget the way you have defended me and taken my part, even risked your life, when Simon was trying to play Robin Hood — and all so that you could establish a marriage which I am sure you must bitterly regret."

"No, I don't regret it, and if I have done anything to make you think so, I am very sorry."

"It is a most unprofitable match," she persisted. "To you, I mean. All the advantages are on my side. You stand to gain nothing."

"Tamsin, that is nonsense. I have gained you."

She glanced at him, uncertain, not daring to take this too literally. He had perched himself on the edge of the table, his long legs crossed. His hair was ruffled, the usual dark lock fell across his forehead. He shook it back, a familiar gesture: everything about him was familiar, yet he was different, older and harder. How could she count on anything the young, impulsive John had said before he had measured the consequences — and before she had written him that letter?

"Do you still want me?" she whispered.

John looked straight at her and said briefly, "Yes."

"I have treated you abominably," she said, "besides separating you from your friends, and getting you exiled from the Court. I ought never to have accepted you. I ought to have foreseen what would happen and sent you away."

"You have been paying too much attention to my cousin's gloomy predictions, which were designed simply to alarm you. I shall not lose a friend worth having, and as for keeping clear of the Court for a season, I would rather be with you at Crossingbourne than anywhere else in the world."

"It is kind of you to say so."

How long could he bring himself to say such things, even in pretence? How long could the feeling he had for her survive when there was nothing else, from his standpoint, to make their marriage worthwhile? It would be desolating when he began to tire of her, and wouldn't that happen all the sooner if they were isolated and shut up together in a state of banishment?

He had been watching the shadows of doubt and apprehension in her face.

"You are mistaken," he said. "That was not a piece of idle gallantry. It's true that I want to have you to myself in a place of our own, nothing strange in that. But it's not the chief reason I want to go to Kent. Thanks to you, I am at last making my escape out of the land of Egypt, out of the house of bondage. I shall be far freer with you at Crossingbourne than I should have been disporting myself at Whitehall or going to Venice with Robert Evesham."

"What do you mean?"

He gave her one of those brilliant glances, full of gaiety and triumph. "I am my own master at last. Oh, not legally for another two years, but in fact I am now standing on my two feet, which I never did before. Today I was shamed into doing for your sake what I never had the courage to do for myself: to brave my guardian's anger and to challenge his authority — and I have won my battle; I can go to Crossingbourne and learn to manage my affairs like a man, instead of being eternally coerced and cosseted as though I was a child in leading-strings. And this is all due to you, my darling. If I had not met you, I might have gone meekly on for years doing what Bernard told me. I might never have had the guts to break away."

Tamsin heard this with a frowning concentration. When she finally made sense of it, she was so surprised that she had to ask him outright, in case she had misunderstood.

"John, were you *afraid* of Sir Bernard?"

He made a wry little grimace. "Until

today. I had never outgrown my childish fear of him. Can you imagine anything more contemptible? And it's not as though he was unduly harsh towards me. Poor Bernard, the model of a Christian gentleman, I should not like you to think ill of him on that score. No, it was his very perfections that overwhelmed me. He was such a paragon, one of the few people I respected and admired when I was a boy, and the only one I couldn't get round with my blandishments. The dread of his condemnation has continued ever since to thwart my purpose and fetter my will. What a lily-livered coward you must take me for! I wonder if you can believe that there are circumstances when mere spoken anger can be a punishment that is almost too heavy to bear."

"Oh yes," said Tamsin softly, "I can believe that."

How else did he think his own anger had affected her in the last three days?

She was hastily re-interpreting a great many incidents in the light of what he had just told her. Those times when she had considered him indifferent or specious or two-faced or arrogantly self-centred. It now turned out he had been beset by troubles she had never dreamed of. She had been easily misled by the superb young man who seemed to her simplicity so worldly and assured, obliged to submit to his guardian's judgment where legal formalities were concerned, but nothing else. Now she tried to imagine the young man as a little fatherless boy, spoilt and petted yet essentially lonely, coming into the orbit of his impressive cousin, and never able to forget the emotions of dependence and awe that were engraved on his mind then. She wondered why she had been too stupid to guess that there must be something like this in his attitude to Sir Bernard.

"All the help I gave you was to make matters worse by my continual scolding," she said regretfully. "I wish I'd held my tongue."

"It was my own fault for placing you in such an invidious position. What right had I to marry you when I was totally unfit to take care of you in any way? I gave you neither protection nor consequence nor money, nor a roof over your head, not even the use of my name. When I read your letter I suddenly saw how low I had sunk, and what a despicable creature I was. Your suspicions were unfounded, but in fact I *had* deceived you to gain my own ends, for I am sure if you had known the true facts you would have refused to marry me. Your view of liars and braggarts was plain in every line you wrote."

"I beg of you, don't speak of that hideous letter. I was going to ask — I hope you will have the charity to burn it."

"Very well," he replied gravely, "provided you can burn from your memory everything I said to you that night in the wood."

"I gave you plenty of cause to reproach me."

"But not in those terms. I was cruelly unkind to you, my poor girl. I could not, at that moment, forgive you for having forced me to see my own actions in their true light. Afterwards, when I longed to be reconciled with you, it was impossible, for I had decided by then that I must not ask for any return of your trust and affection until I was capable of doing so openly, with my guardian's knowledge, if not with his consent. All through our ride yesterday I was wondering whether I'd manage to tackle him. I wasn't sure, you see. That's the true reason why I wanted you to stay in the same room with us. I need you to stiffen my resolve. I hoped that the fear of disgracing myself in front of you might cast out my fear of Bernard."

Something had stiffened his resolve to the point where it was absolutely inflexible; she did not know whether it was her being there or not.

She said, "I thought you had come to hate me."

"I am just learning properly to love you."

Tamsin felt her heart pummelling so hard against her ribs that she seemed to be suffocating.

John stood up. "Come here," he said, "my dear life."

And then she was across the room and in his arms without knowing she had moved; he was kissing her eyelids and her mouth and her throat and she was clinging to him laughing and crying.

She heard herself saying, "I'm so happy."

"Is that what makes you weep, sweet fool?"

She mopped her eyes and gazed up at him. Her doubts had fled. That moral self-conquest, made in order to vindicate her and save their marriage, had not been simply the result of a scrupulous sense of duty. John said he loved her, and he had proved that he knew what love entailed.

He raised her left hand and brushed it gently against his cheek. Then, letting her go, he fetched a taper from the chimney-piece and held open the door.

It was late and the great hall was dim, though there were a few lights kept burning all night, and they could hear the cough and shuffle of men on guard somewhere out of sight. Tamsin was no longer oppressed by the warlike severities of Laleham. She was no longer frightened by the prospective splendour of Crossingbourne. She could even contemplate going to Minton and being made frostily welcome by Lady Kettering, though she did hope they would not have to stay more than a week. Wherever they were, John would take care of her. She would never be alone again.

They came to the staircase that Simon had fallen down so dramatically a few hours ago. It was not easy for two people arm in arm to climb the spiral stair, especially when one was carrying a candle and the other wearing a farthingale. John and Tamsin contrived to do it, in a leisurely way, because they kept having to stop and explore the fascinating topic of who was the most in love.

Triangles of moonlight shone in through the narrow stone window-slits, giving dizzy glimpses of a silver-washed countryside as they climbed higher and higher in the tower. Most of the inhabited part of the Castle overlooked the courtyard, but this turret was on the perimeter, and the great sweep of land that lay below was rustling with life on the hot August night. There were poaching foxes abroad, and owls, and somewhere out there in the anonymous darkness there must be lovers meeting: a couple lying in the deep grass perhaps, or a woman creeping down to slide back the bolt of a door, a man riding through the trees.

The vigil of a girl waiting and waiting, gradually sinking into despair — then a low whistle, the running together in the shadows, the urgent pleasure, and the minutes staved off against daylight and parting and the long dull pain.

John and Tamsin were too happily absorbed to conjure up such scenes, which they had thankfully exchanged for the lawful freedom of the state apartments. A time would come, about fifteen years ahead, when a swarm of young Harcourts would be entranced by a suitable censored account of their parents' secret marriage. By then they would enjoy telling the story, just as mariners enjoyed describing the rigours of a stormy voyage once they were safe in port. There would be a lively amusement in remembering, and some incredulity. (Could we have done that?) And certain episodes might have a little extra glory added in the telling. But neither John nor Tamsin would ever seriously wish to go back to the past. There would be no incentive; they would not suffer from the sad longings of those who know that the best of their marriage was over almost as soon as it began.

For them the nightingale would continue to sing, in a house that would never become a cage.

Note

Sweet Nightingale is a very old West Country folk song, once a favourite of the Cornish tin miners. It has the same tune as the Somerset Sheepshearing Song.

The words that survive today were printed by Baring-Gould in *Songs and Ballads of the West*; he got them from Bickerstaff's ballad opera 'Thomas and Sally' (1760). Some of the lines in this version are rather commonplace, and there is obviously a chunk of the story missing between the third and fourth verses.

Here, all the same, is the essential core of a popular song which any pair of young lovers might have known at the end of the sixteenth century:

My sweet heart, come along, don't
  you hear the fond song
The sweet notes of the Nightingale
  flow?

Don't you hear the fond tale of
   the sweet Nightingale
As she sings in the valleys below?

Pretty Betty, don't fail, for I'll carry
   your pail
Safe home to your cot as we go;
You shall hear the fond tale of
   the sweet Nightingale
As she sings in the valleys below.

Pray let me alone, I have hands
   of my own,
Along with you, Sir, I'll not go
To hear the fond tale of the sweet
   Nightingale
As she sings in the valleys below.

Pray sit yourself down with me on
   the ground
On this bank where the primroses
   grow.
You shall hear the fond tale of
   the sweet Nightingale
As she sings in the valleys below.

The couple agreed and were married
   with speed

And soon to the church they did
go.
No more's she afraid for to walk
in the shade
Nor sit in those valleys below.

THE WILDERNESS WALK
Sheila Bishop

Stifling unpleasant memories of a misbegotten romance in Cleave with Lord Francis Aubrey, Lavinia goes on holiday there with her sister. The two women are thrust into a romantic intrigue involving none other than Lord Francis.

THE RELUCTANT GUEST
Rosalind Brett

Ann Calvert went to spend a month on a South African farm with Theo Borland and his sister. They both proved to be different from her first idea of them, and there was Storr Peterson — the most disturbing man she had ever met.

ONE ENCHANTED SUMMER
Anne Tedlock Brooks

A tale of mystery and romance and a girl who found both during one enchanted summer.

CLOUD OVER MALVERTON
Nancy Buckingham

Dulcie soon realises that something is seriously wrong at Malverton, and when violence strikes she is horrified to find herself under suspicion of murder.

AFTER THOUGHTS
Max Bygraves

The Cockney entertainer tells stories of his East End childhood, of his RAF days, and his post-war showbusiness successes and friendships with fellow comedians.

MOONLIGHT
AND MARCH ROSES
D. Y. Cameron

Lynn's search to trace a missing girl takes her to Spain, where she meets Clive Hendon. While untangling the situation, she untangles her emotions and decides on her own future.

NURSE ALICE IN LOVE
Theresa Charles

Accepting the post of nurse to little Fernie Sherrod, Alice Everton could not guess at the romance, suspense and danger which lay ahead at the Sherrod's isolated estate.

POIROT INVESTIGATES
Agatha Christie

Two things bind these eleven stories together — the brilliance and uncanny skill of the diminutive Belgian detective, and the stupidity of his Watson-like partner, Captain Hastings.

LET LOOSE THE TIGERS
Josephine Cox

Queenie promised to find the long-lost son of the frail, elderly murderess, Hannah Jason. But her enquiries threatened to unlock the cage where crucial secrets had long been held captive.

THE TWILIGHT MAN
Frank Gruber

Jim Rand lives alone in the California desert awaiting death. Into his hermit existence comes a teenage girl who blows both his past and his brief future wide open.

DOG IN THE DARK
Gerald Hammond

Jim Cunningham breeds and trains gun dogs, and his antagonism towards the devotees of show spaniels earns him many enemies. So when one of them is found murdered, the police are on his doorstep within hours.

THE RED KNIGHT
Geoffrey Moxon

When he finds himself a pawn on the chessboard of international espionage with his family in constant danger, Guy Trent becomes embroiled in moves and countermoves which may mean life or death for Western scientists.

TIGER TIGER
Frank Ryan

A young man involved in drugs is found murdered. This is the first event which will draw Detective Inspector Sandy Woodings into a whirlpool of murder and deceit.

CAROLINE MINUSCULE
Andrew Taylor

Caroline Minuscule, a medieval script, is the first clue to the whereabouts of a cache of diamonds. The search becomes a deadly kind of fairy story in which several murders have an other-worldly quality.

LONG CHAIN OF DEATH
Sarah Wolf

During the Second World War four American teenagers from the same town join the Army together. Forty-two years later, the son of one of the soldiers realises that someone is systematically wiping out the families of the four men.

THE LISTERDALE MYSTERY
Agatha Christie

Twelve short stories ranging from the light-hearted to the macabre, diverse mysteries ingeniously and plausibly contrived and convincingly unravelled.

TO BE LOVED
Lynne Collins

Andrew married the woman he had always loved despite the knowledge that Sarah married him for reasons of her own. So much heartache could have been avoided if only he had known how vital it was to be loved.

ACCUSED NURSE
Jane Converse

Paula found herself accused of a crime which could cost her her job, her nurse's reputation, and even the man she loved, unless the truth came to light.